CAMP
AVERAGE

For Ange and Reg

Text © 2019 Craig Battle

Owlkids Books acknowledges the financial support of the Canada Council for the Arts, the Ontario Arts Council, the Government of Canada through the Canada Book Fund (CBF) and the Government of Ontario through the Ontario Media Development Corporation's Book Initiative for our publishing activities.

Published in Canada by
Owlkids Books Inc.
1 Eglinton Avenue East
Toronto, ON M4P 3A1

Published in the United States by
Owlkids Books Inc.
1700 Fourth Street
Berkeley, CA 94710

Library of Congress Control Number: 2018946402

Library and Archives Canada Cataloguing in Publication

Battle, Craig, 1980-, author
    Camp average / Craig Battle.

ISBN 978-1-77147-305-7 (hardcover)
    I. Title.

PS8603.A878C36 2019   jC813'.6   C2018-903749-0

Edited by Karen Li
Designed by Aldo Fierro/Alisa Baldwin

Manufactured in Altona, MB, Canada, in November 2018, by Friesens Corporation
Job # 246089

A   B   C   D   E   F

Publisher of Chirp, Chickadee and OWL
www.owlkidsbooks.com

Owlkids Books is a division of Bayard
CANADA

CAMP AVERAGE

CRAIG BATTLE

Owlkids Books

TABLE OF CONTENTS

CHAPTER 1

"WE'RE NUMBER TWO!"

It was late June, as always, when the buses arrived.

The yellow seventy-two-seaters screamed down the bumpy, potholed dirt road into camp, their big black tires crunching the stray bits of gravel underneath. And from inside them came a loud and unmistakable chant: "We're number two! We're number two!"

The buses stopped in front of a squat brown building marked "Office," and nearly two hundred boys streamed out. The campers kicked up clouds of gray dust and shouted at one another, pointing out familiar things: The baseball diamond! The mess hall! The cobwebs above the mess hall doors!

Welcome to Camp Avalon (or Camp Average, as it's known to kids far and wide), on the shores of Oak Lake.

A gang of counselors in bright orange camp T-shirts yanked the boys' bags off the buses and then descended on the kids themselves.

"Mini campers! If you're seven or eight years old, come this way!" one hollered, beckoning the smallest kids around the side of the office and down the hill to their cabins.

"Senior campers!" another counselor shouted. "Wait up!"

Many of the seniors, all between thirteen and fifteen years old, had been coming to Camp Average for years. They were already halfway to the green clapboard buildings they'd call home for the next six weeks.

Everyone left was a junior camper. Eleven-year-old Mackenzie Jones stood in the dirt with a duffel bag at his feet. While counselors confirmed arrivals and offered cabin assignments to kids who already knew them from letters they'd received that spring, he tilted back his mop of brown hair, squinted his green eyes up at the skyscraper-less sky, and took a deep breath of wet lake air into his lungs.

"Mack!"

A beaming, sporty kid with dark skin and black eyebrows pushed through the shuffling crowd—Andre Jennings, Mack's best camp friend. As soon as he was close enough, the two launched into the Camp Average handshake they'd invented the year before: a high five followed by a kind of full-body shrug.

"How was the school year?" Andre asked. The two had

texted back and forth between September and June, but they'd shared more slam-dunk highlights and wipeout videos than actual information.

"Good," Mack replied. "Got a B in … something. Yours?"

"Good as ever."

"New A's lid." Mack directed an upward nod at the brand-new green-and-yellow Oakland Athletics hat atop Andre's head. It was the fifth version of the same design he'd been wearing since they met as seven-year-old mini campers.

"You know it." Andre grinned as he ran his thumb and index finger along the brim. "Gotta keep it fresh!"

"Miles is around here somewhere," Mack said, referring to a school friend who'd been on his bus. As he spoke, he began casually stretching out his quadriceps, balancing on his right leg and pulling his left foot behind him, then switching. "Wi-Fi come with you?"

"Nah," Andre said, turning his hat backward and jogging in place. "He gets carsick on long bus rides."

Just then, Willy "Wi-Fi" Reston's parents' station wagon pulled up and out popped Andre's friend from home. He dragged his duffel bag out of the back of the car and slammed the door behind him.

"Guys, you won't believe how much tech I fit in here!"

he yelled. "We're *set*."

"Later, man!" Andre fired back urgently. He got into a half crouch and looked at Mack, whose game face was plastered on. "We all caught up?"

"Yup," Mack replied.

Once the counselors saw Wi-Fi and had checked him off their sheets, all of junior camp had officially been accounted for.

"Okay, everyone," a counselor shouted over the fray. "You're good to head off to your—"

His voice might as well have been a starter's pistol. Mack and Andre bolted off the dirt road and onto the clipped green grass, leading a hundred-kid charge to the cabins on the other side of the main field.

Out of the blocks, Andre was winning by a step or two, so Mack put his head down and pushed harder. They were both gunning for cabin 10, because the first kid there got first pick of beds, and Mack didn't want to get stuck sleeping next to a counselor.

He inched into the lead when Andre slowed to look at the pandemonium behind them, then Mack took all three stairs to the door in a leap and slammed his shoulder into the old wooden structure to stop himself, nearly taking it down with him.

"Okay," he said, catching his breath, "that's the last

time I try that hard all summer."

Mack yanked open the door to reveal a small, spare room: three sets of bunk beds for campers down the left side, another set sandwiched between two single beds for counselors on the right side, and a tiny bathroom at the back. He sprinted straight for the bunk bed halfway down on the left, one that carried a special distinction: it was technically farthest from adult supervision.

As the other kids swarmed into the room, Mack climbed up to the top bunk and lay back on its crinkly vinyl mattress, putting his hands behind his head. Looking up at the plain brown plywood walls, ceiling beams, and rafters, which hadn't been touched since he started coming here—maybe since his *dad* came here—he felt the entire camp experience come back to him all at once. He closed his eyes and was briefly transported down to the waterfront on the opposite side of the office, where his life jacket and water skis awaited.

As a junior camper, he'd earned the right to make his own schedule, and the one he'd roughed out on the piece of yellow foolscap paper now stashed in his shorts pocket included a ton of water sports.

"Hope you don't mind sleeping with a foot in your back!"

Mack snapped out of his daydream as something

jabbed his mattress from below, and he found Andre gleefully kicking the underside of his bunk. Mack looked around and saw that every spot but one—the lower bunk between the counselors' beds—was filled. That last spot went to Miles Holley, who walked into the cabin looking as if he hadn't even bothered to break a sweat.

His face partially hidden behind glasses with thick black frames, Miles was carrying a stack of boxed rocketry equipment he'd evidently couriered to the camp office.

"Rocketry?" Mack asked his friend from school. "Again?!"

"Of course!" said Miles, carefully laying the boxes on his bed. "I'm at skill level three. I'm aiming to hit level four well before average starting age. Now, level five, that's when—"

The door swung open again, and the cabin's two counselors stumbled in, lugging eight duffels with them. They created a gigantic pile in the middle of the floor.

"All right, men," said the older and quite-a-bit-heavier counselor. "Anything left in this pile in sixty seconds is going in the lake."

And just like that, two things happened: first, all eight kids hopped to it, grabbing the bags with their names on them and unpacking the contents into the bins under their beds; and second, the counselor became known as Laker for the rest of the summer. Most of the kids in cabin 10 never even learned his real name.

"Okay, now it's bed-making time," said Laker, still breathing heavily from his exertion. "Camp Director's coming around for inspection in ten minutes, and he'll want to see smooth covers and tucked-in sheets."

Once the ten minutes was up, Laker and the other counselor, Brian (who got to keep his name—for now), looked around the room and were pleased with what they saw. That is, until their eyes fell on the lower bunk at the back of the room. The bed was not made, and the dark-haired boy sitting on it appeared to be crying.

"Hey, buddy," said Brian, crouching next to the boy. "What's your name?"

"Patrick Meyer," he said through tears. "My friends call me Pat."

"What's the problem, Pat?"

"Sorry to hold things up. But it's just … I lost my lucky silver dollar when I started unpacking my bag. It belonged to my grandfather. I can't find it anywhere."

Wi-Fi, who had taken the bed above Pat's, stifled a laugh, and Andre rolled his eyes, but neither Laker nor Brian seemed to notice.

"Okay, everyone!" Laker said. "You heard Pat! Look under your feet. Find that dollar."

The search started slowly, with just the two counselors and a new kid Mack didn't recognize—he'd chosen the bed above Miles's—helping Pat. Laker scanned the floor, but he didn't find the dollar there, so he pulled out Pat's duffel. Which was empty.

"Maybe it fell into someone else's bag?" Mack offered with a slight grin, drawing a death stare from Miles. Again, the counselors didn't catch on.

"Good call," said Laker. "Bags out! And look under your mattresses while you're at it."

Things escalated quickly from there. As duffels flew out from under beds, one landed on the new kid, who tripped over a mini soccer ball and hit the wood floor with a thud, dumping a handful of change out of his pocket. Suddenly the ground was covered with silver coins—any one of which could have passed for a silver dollar from afar.

"Found it!" yelled Spike, one of the Triplett twins, who had jointly claimed the bunk bed at the front of the room. He quickly stooped to pick up a quarter.

"No, I did!" shouted Mike, his brother, as they bumped heads and hit the floor. The two got up, forgot the coin, and began shouting at each other with clenched fists.

It wasn't long before Wi-Fi and Pat joined the fray— one to shout, "Fight! Fight! Fight!" and the other to dive onto the ground to sift through the lost coins alongside their rightful owner. Andre stepped in between the twins while Mack picked up a random duffel bag and emptied it onto the cabin floor.

"No silver dollar!" he shouted. "But, hey, who wears teddy-bear pajamas?!"

Just then, the longtime junior-camp director, Simon Yang, appeared in the doorway to find all the mattresses turned over, the beds unmade, duffel bags hanging from all corners of the room, a couple of dozen coins rolling around on the floor, and eight kids and two counselors engaged in what looked like a bench-clearing brawl between hated rivals.

"Let me guess!" shouted Simon, instantly drawing the attention of everyone in the room. "Pat lost his fifty-cent piece?"

"Silver dollar, sir," Pat corrected him.

"Oh right, silver dollar," said Simon. "We seemed to go *all last summer* without finding that particular coin, didn't we? Almost like *it never existed in the first place!*"

It dawned on Laker and Brian: they'd been pranked.

The embarrassed, exasperated looks on their faces were all the payoff Pat needed.

"It's going to be a great summer," he said as Simon pulled the two counselors outside for a talk.

Yes, it is, Mack thought.

CHAPTER
2

"WHO'S THE NEW GUY?"

The eight residents of cabin 10 spent the afternoon undoing the damage from Pat's prank, sorting out the mess on the floor and remaking their beds. They finished just in time to hear the dinner bell ring out over the loudspeakers placed around the camp and inside each building.

The boys cut diagonally across the field outside their cabin, passing by the backstop at the far corner. When they approached the metal flagpole at the bottom of the grassy hill by the mess hall, they saw a counselor on a ladder busily trying to untangle a homemade Camp Average banner from the branches of a nearby pine tree.

"My money's on the tree," Pat joked as they watched the counselor try to pull the flag down without tearing it in half or losing the sewed-on black *A* at the center of the design. "Or, I mean, it would be if I could only find my silver dollar." He patted himself down.

"Too soon!" Andre said, giving him a light push.

The rest of the counselors were organizing kids into lines, with the seven-year-olds from cabin 1 starting things off.

Mack was leading the cabin 10 campers as they closed in on their place, but at the last second, Andre cut in front to beat him to the spot.

"First in line means first to the meatballs," Andre said, pumping his fist and licking his lips.

"Everyone knows they get better with age," Mack replied, shrugging like he didn't care about being second.

Coming in last was the new kid, and Mack seized the chance to size him up. He was wearing a stiff, expensive yellow polo shirt and khaki shorts, and his black hair was carefully gelled and parted over his left eye. At first glance, he looked like he had more in common with the counselors than the campers.

"Who's the new guy?" Mack whispered to Miles as they waited for their line to get called in for dinner.

"You're kidding, right?" Miles replied, mouth agape.

"No. What do you mean?"

"That's Nelson Ramos—as in, *the* Nelson Ramos," Andre chimed in. "Nelson's New Toys? Nelson's Next-Level Gaming?"

"They're two of the most popular YouTube channels in

the world!" Miles exclaimed. "*Everyone* knows who he is."

That's when it clicked. Of course Mack knew who Nelson Ramos was. If you'd ever been on the internet, you'd seen an episode of Nelson's New Toys. The star of the channel had unboxed everything from remote-controlled drones to vintage action figures—and reportedly made a pile of money in the process. And as he got older, he'd added a second channel for gaming, meaning his mini empire grew along with his audience.

But still, Mack gave himself a free pass for not immediately recognizing the YouTube celebrity. In Nelson's videos, he was always leaning into the camera, smiling and doing voices and making sound effects. In real life, he was standing two feet from the closest person and making eye contact with nobody.

"What's he doing here?" Mack asked his friends as their line started to move.

"Camping, one would assume," Miles deadpanned.

"Well, obviously. But what's he doing *here*? Rich kid like that, he could afford to go anywhere."

Mack's question was quickly forgotten as the lines finally started to move. Inside the mess hall, the boys rushed down the steam-table line and grabbed plates heaped with spaghetti, meatballs, and garlic bread. Fifteen minutes later they were full and dozy, ready for evening activities. And on the first night of camp, that always meant one thing: movie night in the lodge next to the office.

But before that could happen, it was time for speeches. And that always meant something else: a recounting of the 1951 All-Camp Junior Baseball Tournament.

"Hello, all," said Simon, the junior-camp director. He had short dark hair that was just starting to gray, wire-rimmed glasses, and a runner's body without an ounce of fat on it.

"Hi, Simon!" roared the campers, many of whom were wearing their orange camp T-shirts.

"I'd like to tell you—particularly the new guys—a story. And I mean, it's hard to believe it was just sixty-eight years ago this month that the famous baseball tournament began ..."

Shouts of "Oh no!" and "Come on!" and "Not again!" rang out as Mack and the rest of the campers in the mess hall playfully protested the story. But Simon only smirked as he carried on.

"Now, though it may look like it"—Simon ran his hand over his head to reveal a receding hairline—"I *wasn't* actually alive for the game. But I know everything there is to know about it. Camp Avalon was the underdog against Killington in the 1951 all-camp final. No, sir.

No one gave our forebears much of a shot."

"But we gave them a shot in the arm!" Mack chanted along with his fellow campers.

"What, you know this story?" Simon asked with a furrowed brow, drawing chuckles from the crowd. "It's true, though—we did give them a shot in the arm. Ol' Bucky Brisker hit a massive home run for Avalon that day. Jimmer Nicholson pitched a two-hitter through eight innings to take a four to one lead into the bottom of the ninth."

Simon turned and looked up at a lone black-and-white picture hanging above the steam table. It was the 1951 team—all of them eleven or twelve years old, white uniforms caked in dirt, ball caps on, arms around each other's shoulders.

At cabin 10's table, Mack looked around at his roommates. Miles was nose-deep in a thick hardcover called *Fundamentals of Aeronautical Engineering*, while Andre sat on the edge of his seat, hanging on every word, even though he'd heard this story at least as many times as Mack had.

"Jimmer, he had this nice sidearm delivery," Simon continued, winding up and flinging an imaginary pitch. "Yeah, he was tired by then, but he had fight and a three-run cushion. He got two outs on hard-hit grounders, but then he gave up a walk. And then another walk. And then *another.* Bases were loaded …"

Simon stopped for the most dramatic of pauses.

"… for Crushin' Cal Newburg."

"Boo!" Mack and everyone else shouted.

"Why'd they call him Crushin' Cal? 'Cause he hit more homers than most guys had at bats that summer. He'd already had a single and a double that game, and he'd cashed in the lone Killington run. He stepped up with that menacing stance, crowding the plate like crazy, knowing that one swing would win the tournament for Killington."

Simon mimicked the stance and waved an invisible bat above his head.

"Jimmer was shaken. He threw the first pitch in the dirt. Ball. Two more in the dirt. Balls two and three. One more ball and he'd walk in a run. He had no choice—he had to challenge Cal."

Mack looked again at the boys sharing his table. Andre was practically kneeling on the floor in front of his chair, and Miles's book was nowhere to be seen. Even the kitchen staff had gathered in the steam-table window to catch the ending.

"He threw a rising heater, top of the strike zone. Crushin' Cal hauled back and swung with everything he had. And he hit it a mile …"

Simon swung his imaginary bat and looked out into

the distance as if following the ball. Then he tilted his head back.

"… straight up in the air."

"Yeah!" Mack cheered as the camp erupted.

"Jimmer called for it and caught the final out of the game. Avalon 4, Killington 1."

Simon took another look back at the team photo as the whooping died down.

"Maybe we'll see another team like that at this year's junior tourney, huh? And hey—"

"We're due!" yelled the campers.

Mack clapped Andre on the shoulder, and the baseball fanatic blushed as he slid back into his chair.

"And with that, I have just a bit of news," Simon said. "I have taken the position of senior-camp director, so I am no longer the director of junior camp. That position now belongs to Winston Smith, who you juniors will meet tomorrow. Now let's get our movie on!"

What? Mack craned his neck to scan the room. *Winston who?*

As Simon walked off, a blond-haired man in a black tracksuit stood up from the directors' table. He flexed his biceps like a body builder and pointed out at the crowd of boys, drawing a few laughs, then sat back down. And that was it. No ceremony. No speech.

Mack hadn't read every line in the pre-camp material sent to his house, but he prided himself on his knowledge of the place. How did he not know about *this*?

Hours later, everybody else in cabin 10 seemed to have moved on from the big news, but a strange feeling stuck with Mack. It was after lights-out, a time when most counselors disappeared, leaving just a few on cabin porches to make sure no one snuck out—or maybe to help a kid who needed it.

As Wi-Fi, the cabin tech wizard, passed out the latest Nintendo DS games he'd stuffed into his duffel bag, Mack pumped his fellow cabinmates for information by flashlight.

"What do you guys know about the new junior director?" he asked. "He seemed a little insc ... inscrow ... anybody got a dictionary?"

"I think the word you're looking for is 'inscrutable,'" said Miles, who was lying in bed and reading his rocketry manual using a book light.

"Right, inscrutable," said Mack. "Hard to read. People laughed when he did that flexing routine, but I don't think he was joking."

"Ah, he seemed all right," Andre said, grabbing a game called *Mashy Masherson's Great Big Mashfest* from

Wi-Fi's stash.

On his upper bunk across from Mack's, Nelson Ramos lay quietly with his hands behind his head.

"What do *you* know, new guy?" Mack asked, shining the flashlight on him.

Nelson looked over with a straight face. Then he shrugged his shoulders, popped two green earplugs into his ears, and turned to face the wall.

"Exactly!" said Wi-Fi. "He's not 'inscrutable' or whatever, just a boring adult. There's nothing *to* know."

"Yeah, maybe," Mack said, unconvinced.

"Right," Pat added. "I mean, how bad could he be?"

CHAPTER 3

"HOPE YOU LIKE PRUNES"

The next morning the boys of cabin 10 woke up early. The second he opened his eyes, Mack pulled off his socks and held them over his head. Almost immediately, six other pairs of socks went up in the air as well (everybody's but Nelson's).

Mack sat up silently and looked over at Laker. He could do this. He could put both of his socks on his counselor's head without waking him up, a first-morning tradition dating back to ... well, maybe even before Camp Average's last baseball tournament win.

Mack slowly climbed down from the top bunk and his feet made soft padding noises as they touched the floor. It occurred to him that having socks on would have actually dampened the sound a bit, but oh well—there was always next year.

He crept to the back of the room, where Laker was asleep in his bed next to Miles and Nelson's bunk. The new kid was peering down, a look of confusion on his face. He was about to say something when Mack put a finger to his lips.

Just then, Laker rolled over to face Mack.

"It's all over!" Miles whispered, before clapping a hand over his mouth.

Miraculously, though, Laker didn't wake up. Mack stood next to the bed, taking a wide stance to make sure he didn't slip. The first two socks were key. They were the only ones that actually had to touch the counselor's head. If they went on, the others just sat on top of them. But delicacy was of the utmost importance.

Mack flicked his arms out a bit, then lowered the first sock onto the side of Laker's head, above the ear. No movement. Success.

But wait! The counselor's face pinched as he wiggled his nose and inhaled deeply.

"Now it's really over!" Again, Miles muzzled himself.

Mack waited and then … Laker exhaled. No more movement. Mack placed the second sock and tiptoed away, a victorious smirk on his face.

Andre and Pat went next. Six socks down.

Spike and Mike made it ten.

Wi-Fi and Miles made it fourteen.

Then, as the seven kids wriggled back into their sheets

to wait for Laker to wake up, they heard two other feet hit the floor.

Nelson's.

Oh no, Mack thought, convinced the new kid was intent on spoiling their fun. But to his surprise, Nelson carefully took off his socks and put them on Laker's head to make it a full house: sixteen socks. The boys did a series of silent fist pumps and air high fives.

Mack grinned at Nelson. If only his YouTube fans could see him now!

It wasn't long before Laker finally came to, his head weighed down by a pile of sweaty cotton and polyester. He recognized the smell before the prank, which he really should've seen coming.

"Ugh, what's … ?" he said. "Hey!"

Brian woke with a start and stood up, looking around. "What? What's going on?" Then he saw Laker shaking socks off his head and howled in laughter.

The rest of the cabin joined him.

"Hey, Laker," Pat squealed between belly laughs as the counselor rushed to the sink at the back of the room to douse his head in water. "Have you seen my socks? I lost those, too!"

Half an hour later everyone from cabin 10 was still buzzing. But the smiles vanished the second the boys arrived for the daily pre-breakfast flag-raising at 7:50 a.m. sharp and saw Winston waiting for them. He was dressed in a light gray hoodie, red short shorts, white-and-red high socks, and old-school black running shoes. The outfit would have been funny if not for the look on the junior director's face: somehow stern, determined, wild, and excited all at the same time.

In previous years at flag-raising, Simon would read baseball scores from the night before, and Andre's whole body would vibrate as he waited for the A's game to be called out. But Winston didn't seem interested in continuing that tradition.

"Okay, men, time for a little introduction," he said, puffing out his chest. "As Simon told you last night, I'm Winston. My parents must have named me that because they knew I'd win a ton!"

Again, it should have been funny, but no one was laughing. Mack and Andre looked at each other, eyebrows raised. Who was this guy?

"I love all sports. Whether it has a puck, racquet, club, wicket—whatever. If you can play it, I'm all over it. When I was your age, I spent more time each day on the baseball diamond than I did sleeping, and I woke up every morning ready to do it again." He appeared to get choked up before collecting himself. "I love baseball, but I love winning even more. And because I love winning, I do it *all the time*. That's what I'm here to teach you."

Sure, sure, Mack thought. *When is waterskiing?*

"But enough about me," Winston continued. "It's time to get to the new rules, which are going to help you all win as much as I do. I've used these on everyone from toddlers to senior citizens, and they are foolproof. First rule: win."

Oh no.

"Second rule: win."

Oh nonononononono.

"Third rule, and this is a new one for me: no more chanting 'We're number two.' From now on, we're number *one*. Anyone caught chanting 'We're number two' does push-ups."

Mack shot a sideways glance at Andre, whose eyes were wide with fear at the direction this was heading.

"Now, I get it. I've looked over some scorecards from recent years." Winston opened his mouth to say something more before he stopped himself. Then he cleared his throat and continued.

"I know we haven't *always* come out on top. In fact, we basically *never* come out on top. But maybe that's because you haven't been channeling your efforts in the right direction. Maybe you weren't fueling yourselves in the proper way or getting involved in the right activities to help you maximize your physical abilities."

Mayday, mayday. This is not good.

"That's why you'll be seeing a lot of healthier fare in the mess hall this summer. No more hot dogs for junior campers. No more sugar cereals. And if you see a pancake, expect a lot of buckwheat to come with it."

Mack looked back at Andre, scrunched up his face, and mouthed the word "Buckwheat?"

Winston continued dropping the hammer. "As you probably already know, I'm also taking control of everyone's schedule."

Mack's right hand formed a fist in the pocket of his shorts, crumpling the yellow piece of paper there into a tiny ball.

"And to help us figure it all out," Winston continued, "you're going to participate in a series of Mandatory Athletic Aptitude Tests, or MAATs. If you profile as a ball-hockey player, we'll get you a hockey stick, and you can have at it—six hours a day, every day. Or if you've got what it takes to swim circles around Michael Phelps, I hope you like prunes because you're going to spend so much time in the pool you'll be pruney all summer!"

Come on! Who likes prunes?!

Finally, Mack could take no more and defiantly raised his hand.

"Sir, uh ... what about non-competitive activities? Like water sports."

"Or rocketry," Miles added, sounding like he already knew the answer.

"Great question. For the time being, those activities are open only to senior campers and mini campers," Winston said remorselessly. "Maybe later in the summer we can talk about a rewards structure of some kind. But until then, it's practice, practice, practice."

Winston said this as if the junior campers had been waiting to hear it all their lives.

Mack's summer flashed before his eyes.

No cannonballs off the dock.

No canoeing.

No waterskiing.

Not even any rocketry.

Just one sport—all day, every day—and he wouldn't even get to pick what it was.

For the next forty-two days.

"Sound good?" Winston asked, expecting a yes.

Minutes later, the boys were in line for breakfast, and the smell of eggs, bacon, and oatmeal with brown sugar and blueberries filled the mess hall. It was supposed to be a send-off to normal camp food, but no one had much of an appetite. Tray in hand, shuffling his feet slowly toward the steam table with his cabinmates, Mack was the first to speak.

"There must be some mistake."

"The new brochures said something about a new, more 'dynamic' attitude, but ..." Miles said.

That's when Mack's eyes fell on Nelson, who seemed to be biting his lip.

"Hey, new ... I mean, Nelson. You know something, don't you?"

Nelson stared at the floor like he was going to say nothing again. Then he looked Mack in the eye. "Yeah, maybe."

"Okay, then. Out with it."

The words came out in a rush. "I went to an info session when I was choosing camps, and the people leading it never said anything about kids making their own schedules. They told us they'd figure out activities once camp started. To tell you the truth, that was actually part of the appeal for me. I get tired of having to make decisions all the time."

Wi-Fi laughed. "What, like having to choose which awesome video game to review?"

"Or where to spend all your sweet, sweet cash?" Pat

chimed in.

Nelson scowled, hardening up again.

"Whatever," he said. "They made my parents sign something saying they were fine with the scheduling." He turned away and walked to the cereal station.

"Wait!" Mack said to the rest of the group, too agitated to notice Nelson's departure. "Did your parents sign anything from camp?"

Everyone nodded.

"Mine did, too. They got a pack of forms in the mail a month ago and sent them back the next day."

"That means—" said Pat.

"They *agreed* to this!" finished Mack. "*We* agreed to this."

Bringing up the rear, Laker overheard him.

"Anything the matter, men?"

"No," Andre said, stepping between Mack and their counselor to grab a banana from a basket on top of the steam table. "Guess he's just not a fan of oatmeal."

CHAPTER
4

"A BETTER, MORE COMPETITIVE YOU"

Founded on a patch of unused lakefront property in 1918 by a couple of well-meaning mythology buffs (Avalon is the name of the island where King Arthur's sword, Excalibur, was forged), Camp Average initially wasn't a sports camp at all. Over the years, the founders added a baseball diamond here, a basketball court there, and suddenly it looked as sports-minded as any camp in its area. And so they went with it.

But if the founders could see it now, they wouldn't recognize it.

After breakfast, Mack and the boys emerged onto the main field to find it had been transformed while they were in the mess hall. Mack thought it looked less like their old camp and more like something straight out of the NFL Scouting Combine, the event where college football players showcase their skills for professional coaches.

There was a makeshift runway for the forty-yard dash. There was a station for measuring the height and reach of each junior camper. There were machines and devices for testing stamina and vertical leap. There were spots for campers to show how far they could throw a baseball, how fast they could smack a slap shot, how many three-pointers they could hit in a row.

Rolled out across the front of the camp office was a large, wrinkled banner that read, "Take It to the MAATs!"

So, Mack thought, *the phrase "Mandatory Athletic Aptitude Testing" isn't just something Winston pulled out of midair.*

But he wasn't impressed. He had no interest in playing Winston's game. And if he didn't show any 'athletic aptitude,' maybe they'd put him as far away from competitive teams as possible—the waterfront would be a good place for that, he mused. Or, better yet, maybe they'd just forget about him altogether.

The boys from cabin 10 crossed the field and approached what looked like the first station. But the guy running it, a senior camper sporting aviator glasses and a buzz cut, held out both hands like a traffic cop to get them to stop. He laid out the basics. First, the boys were getting broken up by last name. Second, they would rotate through the various stations one by one until they were finished.

"Smart," Mack mumbled under his breath. "Divide and conquer. Still not going to work."

The traffic cop asked for their names and told Mack to stay while the others fanned out. Then he measured Mack's height and reach and typed the results into a laptop.

"Whoa!" said the traffic cop.

"What?" Mack asked, sidling up to steal a glance at the computer screen.

"You're five-four with a five-seven wingspan."

"So?"

"That puts you in the ninety-ninth percentile in height for eleven-year-olds. In other words, you're taller than pretty much everyone your age."

"Huh," Mack said, picturing himself towering over ninety-nine percent of the people on the planet.

Next station: baseball throw. Mack grinned as he walked the twenty feet between booths, but then he felt a whoosh of air as someone speed-walked past him.

"Get the lead out, buddy!"

It was Winston in all his short-shorts glory, circling the field with his clipboard like a shark ready to strike. Mack definitely didn't feel like his "buddy."

Sure, the measurement thing had been mildly interesting, but he had no desire to show off his baseball skills for a guy who seemed determined to ruin his summer.

After quickly stretching out his right arm, Mack grabbed a baseball from a giant white laundry basket, stepped up to the designated line, and launched a throw without thinking. The ball rolled to a stop just after it passed the third of the orange cones being used for measurement.

"Looks like about eighty feet. Not too bad," said the tan, muscle-bound senior camper running the station. He was wearing a vintage-looking blue-and-white Brooklyn Dodgers ball cap and had the beginnings of a goatee. "But ..."

"But what?" said Mack.

"Kid in the last group got a hundred and fifty-five."

"Good for the kid in the last group," Mack replied icily.

He picked up a second ball from the basket and threw it aimlessly.

"Looks like ... maybe seventy-five," said the senior camper.

Mack shrugged, grabbed a third ball, and approached the line for a final time.

"Put those throws together," the senior camper joked, "and you match Andre."

"Wait, what?" Mack gasped.

"Andre Jennings," the senior camper read off his clipboard. "Know him?"

Mack nodded, trying to calm his competitive nerves.

Don't do it, don't do it, don't do it, he thought.

"You ready?" the senior camper asked.

"Just a second." Mack put the ball down and stretched again, rotating his arm in a windmill motion, going faster and faster, really giving it a warm-up.

He plucked the ball off the ground and looked out at the field, visualizing where he wanted it to go. He counted six orange cones out to the one hundred fifty mark.

Mack pointed his left shoulder downfield, pulled back his right arm, and then twisted his body into the throw, letting the ball go with all his might. It flew straight with a flatter arc than his first and second tosses and traveled much farther than them, too.

A second senior camper chased after the ball with a tape measure and reported back: 152 feet.

"Shoot!" Mack had missed Andre's mark by three feet. He kicked the grass and looked out at the field like it had sabotaged him somehow, but the senior camper didn't seem to notice.

"Now *that's* not bad," he said.

Mack puffed up his chest.

And baseball isn't even my best sport, he thought as he

walked to the next station, a portable basketball hoop surrounded by a taped-off three-point line.

Andre was just leaving.

"How many'd you make?" Mack asked.

"Ten," said Andre.

"In how long?"

"A minute."

"Okay," Mack said, grinning. "Eleven, here we come!"

Mack had never shot three-pointers from grass before, but the hoop was the same height as the one at his school, and he had no trouble making a practice shot. He set up at the top of the arc so he was facing the hoop straight on, rested the ball in the palm of his right hand, and looked over at the guy running the drill—a senior camper with long blond hair who bore a striking resemblance to Thor.

"Ready?" Thor asked.

Mack nodded.

"Go!"

Mack brought the ball up and fired. It was good. The counselor passed a second ball to him, and he took another shot. Good. As he set up to take his third, he could see out of the corner of his eye that Andre had stuck around to watch. He could also see Winston a few feet behind his friend, keeping tabs.

The third shot: no good.

The fourth: ditto.

He shook his head, put the spectators out of his mind, and took a breath before his fifth attempt. Then he made it.

A bunch of shots later, he was down to just five seconds on the clock.

"One more shot!" yelled Thor.

Mack heaved the ball up and …

"It's good!" the senior camper said. "That's eleven."

Mack pumped his fist and looked over at Andre, who smiled and said, "You got me."

"You got me on the baseball throw," Mack admitted.

The rest of the day was taken up with test after test, with just a break for lunch in the middle. At one station, Mack picked up a hockey stick and took a slap shot that hit thirty-five miles per hour. (It missed the net by several feet.) The senior camper manning that station said his score was okay. At another, he leaped fourteen inches in the air: pretty good. At another, he discovered he had four and a half liters of vital lung capacity: actually kind of amazing.

All the numbers went into a spreadsheet. Mack had no idea why some of them were important, but he was having too good a time trying to beat Andre to care. By the time he'd returned to his starting station, he'd soaked through his shirt with sweat twice over and the day was done.

"I am the champion!" Andre shouted, his arms raised as he met Mack by the measurement station.

"Sure," Mack reluctantly conceded. "At baseball-throw distance, baseball-hitting distance, golf-driving distance ..."

"Basically all the distances," Pat said, coming up behind them with Wi-Fi, Spike, and Mike.

"... and a few other things. But I got three-point shooting and fastest lap in the pool and second place in a bunch of the stuff you won."

"In other words ..." Andre said.

"You're number two!" chanted the boys from cabin 10. "You're number two! You're number—"

SQUEEEEEEEEEEEEE!

The boys covered their ears and looked to the middle of the field, where they saw Winston holding a screeching gray megaphone. The feedback suddenly cut out when he flipped a switch on the device, and then he raised it to his mouth.

"Great day, everyone!" he said, his voice traveling to all points of the camp. "Over the next couple of hours, I'll check the results and figure out exactly how you'll spend every waking minute of the rest of your summer. You'll get your assignments before lights-out. Tomorrow morning, Camp Avalon starts winning again—and you begin becoming *a better, more competitive you.*"

Mack felt sick to his stomach. He'd played Winston's game after all. And he was pretty sure he'd lost.

CHAPTER 5

"I DON'T EVEN KNOW HOW TO PLAY"

By 8:55 that night, the boys of cabin 10 were cleaned up and dressed for bed—though nobody had claimed the teddy-bear pajamas found the day before, which were now flying like a flag from the rafters. While the cabin's two counselors killed the final few minutes before lights-out by listening to music on their headphones, most everyone else was trying in vain to ignore the impending schedule-related doom.

Nelson, for one, lay on his top bunk thumbing a Camp Avalon info guide intended for parents when Wi-Fi leaned up against the bed and casually rested an arm by his feet.

"So … Mr. YouTube," he said, "let me ask you a few things."

Nelson's face went pale as Wi-Fi launched into what seemed like a prepared list of questions.

"Where do you get your consoles and games? Do you

buy them, or do the companies send them to you? Do you get all the way through the games you review? What happens to them when you're done? What's your favorite game? Did you get that one for free? How many—"

The inquisition wasn't over, but Nelson got a reprieve when Laker snorted and woke with a start, having nodded off for a second. Before Wi-Fi could resume his questioning, a single sheet of white printer paper slid underneath the door of the cabin with a slight whooshing sound.

"The assignments," Mack whispered ominously. He was eager to know the results but terrified of having to live with them.

Miles walked over and picked up the assignment sheet, adjusting his glasses.

"Okay, let's see." He sat down on his bed, the rest of the group crowding around him on the floor. "Mack, Andre, Pat, and Nelson: baseball."

"Yes!" Andre said, drawing a look from Mack, who couldn't believe his friend was on board with this. "What? I *like* baseball. If I gotta be stuck with one thing, better that it's something I like. Right, Pat? Right, Nelson?"

"I don't even know how to play baseball," Nelson said, shrugging.

A hush fell over the room as everyone pondered this. *Never played baseball? How's that possible? And if it* was *possible, how'd he get assigned to the baseball team?*

Miles resumed reading.

Spike got ball hockey.

Mike got soccer.

Wi-Fi got basketball.

"And Miles—er, me—I got stats."

"What?" Wi-Fi asked. "Stats? Like, statistics? Numbers?"

It was no secret that Miles was less into sports than a lot of other kids at camp. And if they needed someone to collect numbers on how all the teams were doing, he would be the best pick for the job. Still, he had trouble hiding his disappointment at being left out. Not even last picked—he wasn't picked at all.

Mack looked over at Brian, who had removed his earphones so he could listen in. He thought the counselor might say something consoling, but then the overhead lights abruptly went out.

"Nine o'clock," boomed Laker. He was silhouetted in the cabin's open doorway with his hand on the light switch. "Into bed. *Now.*"

The boys picked themselves up off the floor, slumped to their beds, and climbed under the covers. Brian slipped out the door, and Laker followed, the door creaking its way closed behind them.

"Be good!" Laker yelled, his voice trailing off.

The cabin was silent for a minute as everyone's eyes adjusted to the darkness. Then Andre threw off his covers and stood up.

"That's not cool what they did to Miles," he said. "I'm not on board with that."

"And I'm not on board with ..." Spike began.

"... getting split up from my brother ..." Mike added as both boys jumped to their feet.

"... all day, every day!" Spike finished.

"And why does Nelson have to do a sport he's never played?" Mack leaped to the floor and pulled Nelson clumsily down off his top bunk.

"Winston can't just steal our summer without even considering our feelings!" added Pat as he and Miles joined the fray.

"This is what I've been saying," Mack said. "Winston needs to be stopped!"

"YEAH!" they all screamed.

"And we're going to be the ones to do it!" shouted Mack.

"YEAH!"

"And ... uh ..." Mack was out of things to yell. As they all stood in an awkwardly tight space in the pitch-dark room, no one knew what came next.

Then the counselor from cabin 7 burst through

the door.

"What's all this shouting?" he shouted, half out of breath from running over. "And what exactly are you going to be the ones to do?"

In their excitement, they'd forgotten about the counselors keeping watch outside the cabins. If they were going to fix things, they'd have to be a lot more careful about it.

Also, they needed a plan. But as Mack's cabinmates turned to him with pleading eyes, he realized he didn't have one.

"Nothing," Mack told the counselor, feeling defeated. "Nothing at all."

CHAPTER
6

"BAD DREAM?"

When Mack opened his eyes, he was on a baseball field.

Oh, great, he thought, *they stuck me in right.*

There were people cheering in the bleachers along the first-base line, so Mack knew it was an official game. But there was something wrong with the opposing players. They were sitting in their chain-link dugout, but only because they couldn't stand up—they were too big. They had hulking shoulders and no necks, and their huge arm muscles were practically ripping through the sleeves of their crisp pinstriped baseball jerseys.

The biggest member of the other team squeezed out of the dugout and stood up to full height. He was nearly as tall as the backstop itself. He swung seven bats at a time like they were toothpicks, and he seemed to be staring at something in right field. Mack turned around and saw nothing but an endless expanse of grass.

Then he realized, *Oh, he's looking at me.*

"Take a picture, why don't you!" Mack shouted, then immediately regretted it.

The monster flung away six of his bats, stepped up to the plate, and watched the first pitch go by for a strike. He laughed at it. Then he smashed the next pitch into right field. Mack reached for the sizzling white-and-red sphere, but it burned a hole through his glove.

Mack turned to chase the ball, which was rolling as if it had two hundred horses under the hood. He finally caught up to it, wheeled, and threw, but the ball started to unravel as it bounced toward the infield. By the time Nelson appeared out of nowhere to pick it up, it was just a ball of string.

Which he promptly threw into the stands.

Pat went after it, got distracted by someone's popcorn, and sat down to eat. Andre found what remained of the ball and ran for home, but he got tangled in the string and fell face-first in the dirt as the monster casually crossed the plate.

"Safe!" the umpire yelled.

Mack kicked the ground and turned to look at the scoreboard: Killington 251, Camp Average 0. Top of the first inning.

Then it started to rain.

Mack woke up with a shot, his palms and forehead

sweaty. He was breathing heavily, unable to process the dream and how real it felt.

Miles shone a flashlight on him from his bed, where he'd been reading under the covers.

"Bad dream?" he asked.

Mack thought about it for a second. "No," he said. "An idea."

After breakfast the next morning, Mack, Andre, Pat, and Nelson emerged on the field holding their ball gloves—Nelson's was crisp and shiny, straight from a vacuum-sealed plastic bag, and it had mini wireless speakers sewn into the webbing. When he put it on and pounded his fist into it, a metallic-sounding voice shouted, "Nice catch!" and his face turned beet red.

"Where'd you get that glove?!" Pat asked.

"I don't know," Nelson stammered. "I found it in my garage when I was packing. Stuff just kind of arrives."

Miles trailed along with his new clipboard, about fifty sheets of graph paper, and a retractable pencil on a string around his neck—all of which had been delivered to their cabin that morning.

"We could just not go," Pat said as they walked toward the diamond.

Waiting for them were a handful of kids they mostly

already knew from previous years, as well as Laker, who was doubling as their baseball coach.

"But that would definitely mean a call home to our parents," Miles answered Pat. "And they already said they're fine with the new schedules."

"Plus, if we don't play, they could just send us home," Andre added.

All the blood drained out of Miles's face. "No," he said. "No way. If they send me home, I'll have to spend every day at work with my dad."

"What does he do?" Andre asked.

"Stats," Miles replied somberly.

"Okay, then—not an option," Andre said. "Maybe we could—"

"Steal his short shorts!" Pat looked hopefully at the rest of the group. "Then he'd have nothing to wear! Right, Mack?"

"Yeah, sure," Mack said distractedly as they all filed into a line with the rest of the newly formed baseball team. "Maybe."

"Thanks for finally showing up!" Laker said, then introduced himself by his real name to the campers who didn't already know him. "Now it's your turn. Tell me your name and your usual position."

Laker pointed to a tall, heavy kid with olive skin and

dark curls at the far end of the line.

"Antonio Garcia," he muttered quietly. "First base."

Mack overheard Pat whisper to himself, "Tony. No other nickname necessary."

Next in line stood a smiling boy whose mouth was moving before his turn had even arrived. "Hey, guys, my name is Kevin Chu. I'm a shortstop. I can turn double plays in my sleep. Kind of a pop-up machine at the plate, though, but I'm going to work on that this summer. Anyway, in the field I—"

"Thanks, Kevin," Laker cut in.

"No problem!" Kevin replied.

Pat: "Charleston Chu. No! Special K."

Next in line: "I'm Sanjay Gill. I usually play more cricket than baseball. But I like the infield."

Pat: "Jay Gills Band."

Mack shot him a confused look.

"What, you don't like classic rock?" Pat whispered. "Fine, let's go with Gilla Monster."

"Better," Mack returned.

The next two in line were clearly friends from back home and introduced themselves in tandem: Jayden Marshall and Reilly Hocker, outfielders.

Pat: "Marshall Law and Captain Hock. This is too easy."

Mack and the other boys of cabin 10 came next. When

prompted, Nelson offered only "no position … that I know of." This drew sideways glances from both the coach and Nelson's new teammates.

Laker shook it off to continue his prepared lesson plan. "All right, thanks, everyone. I'm hoping to figure out what kind of players you are today, so let's get right to it. Mack, you're up. Andre's pitching, and Pat's catching. The rest of you shag flies."

Mack put on a helmet and distractedly swung at several offerings from Andre. He fanned on some but knocked a couple of others into the short outfield before giving up the bat to the next hitter.

After that, he headed to the outfield and made plays only on the balls he couldn't otherwise avoid.

If Laker noticed anything odd about Mack's play, he didn't show it. He was too busy watching Nelson. While Mack seemed distracted, Nelson looked lost. And a bit afraid. He dove away from grounders and watched pop flies sail over his head. Even when he chased down a ball, he rarely had the arm strength to get it back to the pitcher's mound. Twice Laker checked his roster to see that Nelson was really supposed to be there.

Then he called him up to bat just as Winston arrived and hunkered down behind the backstop to watch practice.

Nelson stuck the batting helmet awkwardly on his head and tightened the strap so much it looked close to cutting off his circulation.

"Okay … uh, looking good," said Laker, passing him a lightweight aluminum bat. "Step up."

Nelson shuffled over and put both feet on home plate.

"No, um," Laker said, "you need to stand *beside* it."

"Oh." The newbie baseball player looked down at the slab of white rubber. "Which side?"

After another minute, Nelson was standing in the batter's box, left shoulder pointed toward the pitcher, ready to hit right-handed. He took a couple of easy practice swings, his hands nearly halfway up the bat.

"That's … great. Now we'll take some pitches. Just try to make contact."

Andre served up a slow ball down the center of the plate, and Nelson watched it all the way to Pat's catcher's mitt. Then he watched three more go by.

"Nelson … ?" Laker probed.

On the fifth pitch, Nelson stuck the bat out and tapped a dribbling grounder down the first-base line. The team reacted like he'd hit it five hundred feet.

"Yeah, Nelson!" Pat shouted from his catcher's crouch.

Nelson knocked the next pitch slowly back up the

middle. On each successive offering he got a little bolder, and soon he was slapping balls all over the field.

"Okay, Andre, heat it up," said Laker, and the pitcher started throwing harder.

But Nelson got his bat on every ball, whether the pitch was inside or outside, in the dirt or up around his ears.

That's when Winston's strategy started to become clear to Mack, who was still only half-heartedly following the activity on the field. With his gaming experience, Nelson probably had the best hand-eye coordination in camp.

The at bat came to an end amid a chorus of hoots and hollers, and the junior-camp director had a satisfied smirk on his face as he got up and headed for another playing field.

"Okay, team, let's call it a day," Laker said as the boys came in for a water break.

"Huh, that wasn't so—" Pat started to say.

"JUST KIDDING!" the coach interrupted. "We've still got, like, five hours to go. Let's split up into infield and outfield players so we can run some defensive drills."

Mack saw Miles check his watch and wince. It was ten thirty in the morning—not even lunchtime on the first of something like forty straight days of nonstop skills building—and Miles already seemed beyond bored of taking batting-practice stats. He had come to camp expecting rocketry and good times with his friends. Instead, he got spreadsheets.

Mack guessed that kids all over camp were feeling the same way. And if that was true, then maybe …

Suddenly his face broke into a wry smile. *That's it!* he thought.

Or, at least, it had better be.

CHAPTER
7

"GOOD THING WE
WORE BLACK"

The rest of the day played out like this: drills, lunch, drills, dinner, soccer documentary (featuring lots of drills), washup, cabin. Mack barely said a word to anyone from cabin 10 the entire time, but Miles saw him whispering to Kevin Chu, the talkative shortstop on the baseball team, at dinner.

A minute after Laker and Brian left at lights-out, Miles finally confronted his friend, flashlight in hand.

"What's going on?" he said. "You've been acting weird all day."

Mack hadn't even bothered getting under the covers of his bed. He propped himself up on an elbow and looked at his cabinmates as best he could in the dark. "What if I told you guys I have a plan to fix everything?" he asked. "To beat Winston?"

"We'd be in," Miles said.

"It'll be really hard, and we could get in trouble."

"We're in, Mack," insisted Andre from below him on their bunk bed.

The others nodded in agreement. Even Nelson.

"Okay, good." Mack climbed down and grabbed a pair of black running shoes from his bin. "First step, put on something dark. We're leaving."

"What?" Wi-Fi said. "But all my vitamins are in the office!"

"Not *for good*, Wi-Fi—just for the next hour."

The cabin's tech guru exhaled loudly, but his sense of relief didn't last.

"You have a smartphone handy?" Mack asked him.

"What? Me? You know we're not allowed to have smartphones in the cabin!"

"Wi-Fi …" Mack furrowed his brow.

"Okay, okay! I have five."

"Good. Can you bring up a snoring sound effect on a couple of them and play it on a loop?"

Wi-Fi darted for his bunk with a grin. "Is that all?"

"What's this about, Mack?" Miles asked.

"We need to talk." He pulled a black backpack down off his bed and yanked the straps over his shoulders. "I don't trust the counselors, and we saw last night how closely they listen."

"Where are we going?" Pat asked, grabbing his shoes

just as rhythmic snoring noises emerged from two different spots at the back of the room.

"The field house. It's bowling night for the counselors, so most of them will be miles away by now."

"But what about the one on watch?" Andre asked skeptically. "If he's listening closely, won't he notice eight of us leaving the cabin?"

"I've handled that."

As Mack listened at the door, the other seven kids tied their shoes and zipped up their darkest hoodies.

"Maybe we should wait. Talk about this quietly for a second," Miles said, trying to reason with his friend.

"We don't have any time," Mack said ominously.

Miles bit his lip, full of nervous energy. "Why not?"

At just that moment, a voice from four cabins down screamed out, "OOOOOOOOH! I'M FEELING SICK!"

It was Kevin. No, Charleston Chu. No, Special K.

"That's why not," Mack said. "We're on the move."

He poked his head out the door in time to see a counselor bound up the stairs of cabin 6 and run inside. Then Mack slipped out into the night. Reluctantly, the others followed, with Nelson bringing up the rear.

As soon as they climbed down from the porch, Mack took a right, ran around to the back of the building, and waited for the others to catch up. Then they made their way toward the field house along the small pathway between the cabins and a row of trees.

"Mack!" Miles whispered as they neared the last cabin in the row. "Have you forgotten that the office is up here?! They'll catch us for sure."

Miles was right. As they crouched behind the bushes at the end of the path, they were practically blinded by the bright white spotlight on the front of the office.

Once Mack's eyes adjusted, he saw Cheryl, the camp's longtime facilities administrator, sitting outside the office on a white plastic chair and reading a paperback novel—not ten feet from where they were crouched.

"Good thing we wore black," Pat whispered.

"Shhh!" Miles scolded.

But Pat's nervousness was coming out in a torrent of words. "Hey, do you think this is where that expression 'bush league' comes from?"

"Shhhhh!"

"Because we are *not* good at this."

Miles lunged at Pat. "SHHHHHHHHHHH!"

Cheryl glanced up at the rustling bushes. She put her book down and took a step in the boys' direction and was now just three or four more from standing right on top of them. They were goners.

Mack prepared to retreat, hoping they could get far

enough away before she was able to ID them. But then he heard fast-moving footsteps getting closer. Was it the counselor from outside their cabin, alerting the camp office to their disappearance?

Thankfully, no. As Mack motioned for everyone to stay still, a jogger ran into view. Mack couldn't see the runner's face, but he did make out one identifying fashion choice: red short shorts.

"Hi, Winston," Cheryl called out.

Winston! Of all people to save their day, it was the one they were aiming to overthrow.

"Cheryl!" Winston replied, jogging in place. "Just who I was looking for. Do you have that bus schedule I asked about earlier? I want to make sure everything's arranged for when the tournaments start up."

"Sure thing." She led Winston into the office, and the door creaked to a close behind them.

Mack poked his head out of the bushes. No Winstons. No Cheryls. No counselors.

"Follow me," he said.

"As if we had any other choice," Miles said, looking a little green, even in the darkness.

Mack popped out, ran across the road, and snuck down the side of the office with the others close behind. There was just a dark wooded area between them and the field house, and after two minutes of crouch-walking, they were there.

"See?" Mack said as he opened the door to the darkened gymnasium and turned to his cabinmates. "Piece of cake."

CHAPTER
8

"ARE YOU CRAZY?!?!"

Patches of light from the field house windows dotted the gym floor as they crossed it and ducked into the equipment room. Mack closed the door behind them, opened his backpack, and passed out flashlights.

The yelling started immediately.

"What were you thinking?!"

"How about a little warning next time?!"

"Are you CRAZY?!?!"

"No," Mack answered calmly. "I just had a feeling."

"You had a feeling?!"

Mack received enough dagger stares to start a collection. But he coolly said, "With all this shouting, do you see why we couldn't have this conversation in the cabin?"

It was a fair point.

"But why *here*?" Miles asked. "Did we have to run right by the office? And Winston?"

"Can you think of another place? Because I spent the

whole day trying."

Miles took off his glasses and rubbed his eyes. "I'm not done being mad at you, but we're here. Tell us the plan."

Mack boosted himself onto a sturdy ball-hockey net leaning against a wall, then scooted over to make room for Nelson as the others found spots for themselves.

"What does Winston hate more than anything?" Mack asked.

There was a long pause as the members of cabin 10 thought about this.

Pat broke the silence. "Long shorts?" he asked earnestly.

"No!" Mack said. "He hates losing. He nearly lost it during his introduction speech just talking about our old scorecards. In order to break him, we have to lose."

"Wait, weren't we going to do that anyway?" Nelson asked.

"Probably, but not like we're going to lose now. We're going to lose so badly and so publicly that Wins-a-ton will wish he had never been born."

"So he'll be bummed out or whatever," Andre said. "How does that turn into a better summer for us?"

"Don't you see? He's pushing us so hard because he's trying to turn us into mindless winning machines. If we play just mildly poorly or show any kind of potential at all, he'll keep pushing. If we totally stink, he has to either give up altogether or take another tactic."

Mack furrowed a brow at his own words.

"That doesn't sound right," Pat told him.

"Uh, dictionary?"

"Take another *tack*," Miles suggested. "Or *change* tactics."

"Yeah, those," Mack continued. "And either way, that could mean giving us back our normal schedules."

"And what if it doesn't?" Wi-Fi asked.

"Well, at least we'll ruin his summer, too."

"Are only our teams going to lose ..." Spike started.

"... or every team in junior camp?" Mike finished.

"Winston said baseball is his favorite sport, and he spent half the day watching us practice, so losing there is extra important. But it's still gotta be every team," Mack said. "The more evidence he has that we really are Camp Average, the sooner he'll see he's beat."

"Four of you are in baseball, so we can be sure that team will blow," Wi-Fi said. "But what about all the other ones?"

"That's where you come in." Mack looked from Wi-Fi to Spike to Mike. "You need to get your teams onside."

He pulled a sheet of paper from his pocket. On it, he'd written the schedule of games against the other big-time camps in the area.

"The baseball tournament starts later this week and

runs for about two weeks after that. We play at least four games—three in the round robin and one in the play-offs, which we couldn't win even if we were trying. With any luck, that'll be enough to do the trick. There's also a couple of ball-hockey games in there, some soccer games, and a home-and-home basketball set."

Unusually quiet to this point, Andre finally joined in. "Losing *games* is one thing. But we have to do these sports *every day*."

"That actually might work in our favor," Mack said. "The type of losing we want to do is going to take practice. Besides, in a perfect world, maybe Winston will watch the practices and give up hope from those."

"This is all fine and good for kids who got stuck with a sport they've never played," said Andre, getting frustrated, "but I actually *like* baseball. I'm good at it—and so are you and Pat."

"True," Pat concurred.

"What if I don't want to lose at my favorite sport on purpose?" Andre continued. "Especially when we could actually be okay?"

"This isn't about any one of us, Andre. It's about all of us. If we do this right, everyone can be doing what they like by the end of the summer."

"I get that, but still ... remember the Black Sox Scandal?" Andre continued.

"ENCYCLOPEDIA!" Mack yelled, hoping Miles could fill in the context.

"Eight members of the Chicago White Sox baseball team agreed to lose the 1919 World Series on purpose in exchange for money," Miles said. "When people found out, those players were banned from professional baseball for life."

"Well, this isn't like that," Mack replied.

"Why not?" Andre pressed.

"We're not doing it for money. What we're doing isn't sel*fish*—it's self*less*. We just want everyone to have the summer they planned."

Mack pulled Nelson's arm over to look at his smartwatch. It was approaching ten o'clock. He hopped off the hockey net, stood in the center of the cramped equipment room, and put his hand out palm down.

"Who's with me?" he asked.

Miles was the first to stand up.

"I know I'm not part of a team, so it's different for me," he said, putting his hand on Mack's, "but I'll help any way I can. At the very least, we'll give Winston a taste of his own medicine."

Spike and Mike stood up and added their hands in unison.

"We're ..." Mike started.

"… in," Spike finished.

Wi-Fi and Pat followed.

"One condition," Pat said. "If this plan flops, we'll look into stealing the short shorts."

"Deal," Mack said, breaking into a grin.

Nelson looked uncertain, but he climbed down from the net and put his hand in anyway.

"Whatever," he said quietly.

Finally, everyone's eyes turned to Andre, who was sitting on the ground hugging his knees.

After a long minute, he got up and held his hand above his head.

"For the record," he said, "I'm not sure about this. Losing on purpose feels wrong. But I don't have a better plan."

He put his hand down, and his co-conspirators let out a stifled cheer.

"Thanks, guys," Mack said. "This'll work. Trust me." When he checked Nelson's watch again, he realized more time had passed than he thought. "It's 9:57!" he shouted. "Kevin is creating another diversion in three minutes. We have to go."

They all ran across the gym floor. Mack cracked open the field house door and peered outside.

"Coast is clear." He had just lifted his foot to take the

first step out the door when he heard a shout in his ear.

"Wait, wait, wait!" Pat said, causing every hair on the boys' necks to stand straight up.

They turned to look at him.

"Has anyone seen a silver dollar?" he deadpanned. "I dropped mine."

Everyone exhaled sharply and gasped for new breath, their hearts kicking back into gear.

"Pat, I'm going to ring your—" Andre started.

"Save it for the cabin," Mack ordered. "We have to move."

Four minutes later—following another standout acting performance from Kevin—they were back in their bunks.

Mack lay on his back, but he was too wired to close his eyes. Around eleven o'clock, he heard soft footsteps on the porch and expected Laker and Brian to tiptoe in. But the door didn't open.

"Anything to report?" Mack heard someone whisper. It was a deep voice, and he knew right away it belonged to Winston.

"Cabin 10? Not a peep. But man …"

"What?"

"Those kids sure can *snore*."

CHAPTER
9

"WHAT'S A CUTOFF MAN?"

"So, really, how is this going to work?" Pat asked the next morning, once Mack had finished convincing the rest of the baseball team to follow the plan. The players were lined up in left field, waiting for their coach's instructions. "We just don't do the drills?"

"No, we do them—but we do them badly," Mack said. "Follow my lead."

"Okay, listen up!" Laker yelled at his players. "Today we're going to work on fielding balls in the outfield and making relay throws to home. Mack, you'll be the cutoff man."

"No problem," said Mack, standing at the front of the line. "Except for one thing."

"What's that?"

"What's a cutoff man?" He managed to keep a straight face.

Pat chimed in before Laker could get to it. "It's like when

someone swerves in front of you while you're driving."

He jumped out of line and mimicked swerving in front of Mack, bumping him a bit in the process.

"Hey, let's—" Laker began, trying to regain control.

"Oh, my mom *hates* cutoff men," Mack said, cutting him off. "I don't think she'd be happy to hear I went to camp and became a cutoff man."

"Studies on this subject say you don't *become* a cutoff man," Miles added helpfully. He was standing next to Laker with his clipboard in hand. "You either are one or aren't one. Part of it is depth perception."

"DICTIONARY!" Mack yelled, suddenly enjoying both the conversation and its effect on Laker, who was getting visibly more frustrated by the second.

"That's your ability to judge how far away things are from you. Like, if your depth perception isn't good, you might think a car is far away when it's actually much closer," Miles said.

"The more you know!" said Pat, pounding the pocket of his glove. "But hey, let's play some baseball!"

"Um, Pat?" Laker said. "I think you've got your glove on the wrong hand."

"Nope, pretty sure this is right. I'm right-handed, so I'm wearing the glove on my right hand."

"That's a common mistake," Laker said, smiling. "A

right-handed glove actually goes on your left."

"Then this is a left-handed glove?" Pat said.

"No!" Laker lost his cool.

"Am I wearing *my* glove right?" Nelson asked.

Mack looked over. The glove was sitting comfortably on Nelson's left hand. He wasn't sure if Nelson was asking for real or playing along. But in the end, he thought, it didn't really matter.

"Are you right-handed or left-handed?" Pat asked.

"I'm ambidextrous."

"DICTIONARY AGAIN!" Mack yelled.

"He's both-handed," Miles offered.

"Ah. Then you need to flip it," Mack advised.

"Gotcha," Nelson said, taking the glove off and jamming it awkwardly onto his right hand.

As all this was going on, Andre was standing off to the side, red-cheeked, his glove on the proper hand.

Fifteen minutes later, they all had their gloves on correctly, and the drill was finally set to begin.

"Let's skip the cutoff man for now," Laker called. He was standing by home plate, already exhausted. "When I hit the ball to you, just field it and throw it home."

He tossed a ball up to himself and cracked it to the outfield, where Mack was standing at the ready. He caught the ball, reared back, and threw it hard … well over the backstop. It landed off the field and rolled to a stop near the flagpole.

"Nice distance, Mack," Laker said. "Just rein it in a bit for next time."

Nelson grabbed the next one, a purposefully slow roller, and threw it short.

Pat fielded the one after that and threw it like a rocket at vacant third base. ("I thought that was home!")

The next one was Andre's. He snapped it up and threw it weakly—for him—but at least it dribbled to the plate. Grading on the curve, he aced the drill.

The rest of the day passed similarly.

Two-minute setups took at least fifteen. Anything involving equipment became overcomplicated to a startling degree, with players picking up items backward or upside down or wrong-handed.

After lunch, Winston came out to watch for a half hour. Laker upped the shouting and encouragement, putting on a show of motivation for his boss, but it produced no better results. When Mack attempted to kick a pop fly while working on "shoestring catches," Laker threw up his hands and called a water break.

As the players sat behind home plate soaking up the sun, Mack caught a snippet of conversation between

Laker and Winston.

"They can't be that bad in actual games, right?" Winston asked the coach.

"Wrong," Mack said under his breath.

CHAPTER
10

"PLAY BALL!"

It was around two o'clock on a hot, muggy afternoon when Mack and the boys of the junior baseball team arrived at Camp Roundrock for the first game of the All-Camp Junior Baseball Tournament. Situated on the same lake, just a twenty-minute bus trip away, Camp Roundrock was a mirror image to Camp Average.

"If the mirror was set twenty years in the future," Pat joked.

The grounds looked pretty much the same—winding road, trees, grass, hill, lake—and the main buildings were in roughly the same places. But they were modern to the point of looking straight out of a sci-fi novel.

While the cabins at Camp Average looked lived-in and even sagged in spots, the ones at Roundrock were brand new, with big windows and sharp edges. The camp office seemed made entirely of glass, and the gym looked fit for a pro basketball team—not a bunch of tweenagers on summer break.

And that made sense, in a way. Camp Roundrock gave kids the chance to play lots of sports, but it was known for hoops. Four current pros had attended when they were young, and many present-day campers wanted to follow in their size-sixteen footsteps.

In fact, every one of the three other camps in the area had a specialty.

Roundrock had basketball.

Camp Hortonia dominated ball hockey and had produced no fewer than three NHLers.

And Hall of Fame shortstop Jeffrey "Deets" Dietrich used to spend his summers at Camp Killington, which hadn't lost an all-camp tournament since he went there in the eighties.

But that didn't mean other camps had given up trying to pry the trophy away. Not all of the four local camps bothered to compete in every sport, but they all entered the baseball tournament. It'd been around the longest and therefore carried the most bragging rights.

When the Camp Average bus pulled up in front of the blindingly bright camp office, the Roundrock junior baseball team was already out on the diamond, throwing long toss.

"They look … uh," Nelson said, gulping as he peered out the bus window, "big."

It was true. Even their baseball players were perfectly built to play basketball. (Good luck hitting a liner over the heads of the infielders!) Plus, their baseballs had been painted to look like orangey-brown leather.

"If I'm in the ninety-ninth percentile for height, what does that make these guys?" Mack asked.

"One hundred and ninth?" Pat guessed.

Mack had almost started to get nervous about facing them on the field when he remembered their goal wasn't to win. It wasn't even to save face. They could go down by one hundred runs in the first inning, forcing the ump to stop the game, and they'd have absolutely nailed it.

The Camp Average boys dragged their gear onto the field and ducked into the chain-link dugout. They slid onto the solid, new-looking bench to tighten the laces of their cleats and fiddle with their gloves as Miles stood nearby with his pencil and clipboard.

It wasn't lost on any of them that they were wearing orange Camp Average T-shirts and jogging pants while the Roundrock kids were decked out in sharp blue-and-red uniforms with large *R* logos that made them look like superheroes.

But again, Mack thought, *Who cares? We don't want to look good anyway.*

"Okay, men," Laker addressed the team through the chain-link fence. He was standing on the dirt infield, gnawing the inside of his cheek and looking anxious enough for everyone. "We're playing a full nine innings. Mercy rule after seven, but I don't expect—"

Nelson slowly raised his hand.

"What's the mercy rule?" he asked.

"If either team is down by ten or more runs after its turn at bat in the seventh, the ump will call the game. But—"

Again Nelson raised his hand.

"What do you mean by 'call the game'?"

"*End* the game," Laker grumbled. "If anyone is losing by a lot after the seventh inning, the game will be over, and we'll go back to camp on our bus."

Mack hadn't planned on this stream of questions from Nelson, but anything that had this effect on their coach couldn't be bad.

"We good, Nelson?" Laker asked confidently.

Nelson nodded his head vigorously, a nervous smile on his face.

"Yes," he said. "Just ... er, what's an 'inning'?"

Pat saw an opening. "That's like when your belly button kind of looks like a hole. If it sticks out, they call it an 'outing.'"

"NO!" yelled Laker, drawing looks from the opposing dugout. He continued in a sharp whisper. "That's *not* what an inning is. Every baseball game has nine innings. In each inning, both teams get to bat. When each team bats, the players get to keep batting until the other team gets three outs. To get a player out, you can catch the ball he hit before it touches the ground, or tag him with the ball if he's off a base, or touch the base he's going to while you hold the ball so long as he doesn't have a base he can go back to."

There was a long pause as Laker collected himself.

"You know," Mack finally said, "when you say it like that, baseball really is a complicated sport."

"Any questions about how we score runs?" Laker asked Nelson.

"You touch home plate," the toy whiz answered disgustedly.

"What do you take him for?" Pat put his arm around Nelson's shoulder. "An idiot?!"

"Laker … ?" Andre started to say.

"Call me Coach," said Laker, shaking his head.

"Coach Laker, shouldn't we warm up?"

Laker's eyes went as wide as the lake they'd named

him for. "WE FORGOT TO WARM UP!" he shouted. "Get out there and throw some balls!"

But it was too late.

The umpire walked over in his dark gray chest protector and pulled his mask over his face. "Camp Average … er, Avalon? Let's play ball!"

As the visiting team, Camp Average got to bat first, and according to Laker's lineup card, that meant Mack was up.

AVALON!!!

CAMP ~~AVERAGE~~ LINEUP		
1	MACK	2B
2	SANJAY	3B
3	PAT	C
4	ANDRE	P
5	NELSON	RF
6	TONY	1B
7	JAYDEN	LF
8	REILLY	CF
9	KEVIN	SS

Mack grabbed a bat and helmet and grinned at his teammates as he left the dugout.

So many options, he thought as he headed toward the on-deck circle. *Strike out swinging? Strike out looking? Hit a pop-up?*

Mack watched the pitcher warm up. He was tall and threw hard, and his pitches seemed to sink all the way into his catcher's mitt.

Then Mack settled on an idea: *I'm going to smash this thing right into the ground.*

He stepped up to the plate still grinning so much it seemed to unnerve Camp Average's opponents. The pitcher looked around at his infielders, who shrugged their shoulders as if to say, *What does this kid know that we don't?*

The pitcher was so shaken, he threw the first pitch in the dirt, and it bounced across home plate. Ball one.

The next pitch was better but still low. Ball two.

Then it was Mack's turn to strike. Based on the progression of the first two pitches, he knew exactly where the ball was going. The pitcher wound up and threw it to the bottom part of the strike zone, and Mack brought out his home run swing—but by design, he caught just the top of the ball, bashing it straight down in front of the plate. Fair ball.

Mack dropped the bat and turned to run up the first-base line, but the catcher dug the ball out of the dirt and easily threw him out at first.

The boys waited giddily as Mack trotted back to the dugout. He tried to keep a straight face, but he didn't refuse a few subdued high fives. To anyone on the outside looking in, this seemed like the happiest, most supportive baseball team ever. Just not a very good one.

Mack sat down next to Miles, who wrote "2–3" next to his name on the scorecard.

"What's that?" he asked as Sanjay stepped into the batter's box.

"It means you grounded out to the catcher, denoted by the number two, who threw it to the first baseman, number three," Miles answered.

"Where'd you learn all this stuff?" Mack asked while Sanjay watched strike one cross the plate.

"Winston gave me access to the camp directors' library."

Miles passed Mack a heavy volume called *The Ultimate Guide to Scoring Baseball Games.* On the cover was a quote from Jeffrey "Deets" Dietrich—it read, "There's so much info in here! No, really. Like, maybe too much! You guys ever hear of editing?"

"Why is the first baseman number three and not, you know, number one?" Mack continued his interrogation as Sanjay fouled off another pitch.

"The book doesn't say. He just is."

"Who's number one?"

"The pitcher."

"Why?"

"It's baseball, Mack." Miles shrugged. "You just gotta go with it."

Sanjay swung and missed at strike three, and Miles marked a *K* next to his name.

"Why the *K* and not an *S* for 'strikeout'?"

"Because *S* is used for 'sacrifice,'" Miles said. "Hey, do you want to read the book? I finished it last night. It's just here for reference."

While Mack flipped the book over in his hands, Pat took a big cut at the ball and knocked it straight up into the air.

"No, thanks," Mack told Miles as the Roundrock shortstop caught the ball. "I'm good!"

Miles marked a "6" by Pat's name, and the inning was over.

Mack grabbed his hat and glove and walked onto the field along with the rest of his teammates.

"Went for the pop-up, eh?" he asked, intercepting a straight-faced Pat on the way back to the dugout to get his catcher's gear.

"Uh … yeah," Pat said. He gave his head a quick shake and smiled confidently. "It's a classic!"

One minute and ten warm-up pitches later, Andre was ready to go. But he looked back pleadingly at Mack, playing second base, as the first batter left the on-deck circle.

"You got this," Mack said quietly, so only his friend could hear. "Remember, it's for the good of the whole camp."

Andre nodded and turned back to Pat, playing catcher. Instead of putting fingers down as catchers normally do to request specific pitches, Pat was trying to make shadow animals on the dirt. He and Andre had already agreed on a game-long strategy—slow and in the strike zone.

In other words, predictable and perfect for hitting hard.

The first batter hit a sharp grounder that Mack let roll through his legs, turning it into a double.

The second knocked the first batter home with a left-field liner that became a triple when Jayden overthrew second base.

The third hit a home run over the right-field wall, but even if it hadn't gone out, Nelson wouldn't have got to it. His feet stayed firmly planted in the grass as it sailed over his head.

The Roundrock players managed two more runs, but Andre eventually—mercifully—got out of the inning when one kid lined out directly to Tony at first base (he caught it simply trying to save his own life), and two others struck out trying too hard to hit home runs.

One hour, four Roundrock home runs, and nearly countless (though not for Miles) Camp Average strikeouts later, it was the top of the seventh. Mack and Andre sat next to each other and watched Nelson head toward the batter's box.

"This is embarrassing," said Andre, who'd gamely struck out twice so far and was due up third in the inning. "I don't know if I can do this."

"First of all, it's only embarrassing if you care about Roundrock's opinion, and you shouldn't," Mack told him. "Second, you're thinking about this all wrong. You should have fun with this. Make it a game."

"Baseball *is* a game." Andre rolled his eyes. "There are rules and teams and a scoreboard and everything."

"What I mean is, make it a game *within* a game."

Andre scrunched up his face like he'd just sucked on a lemon. "What?!"

"Test yourself to see if you can do stuff—so long as it doesn't help us score runs," Mack said. "Like, how far can you hit the ball foul?"

Andre was left-handed. If he pulled the ball, it would go into foul territory to the right of right field. Both Mack and Andre looked out there simultaneously. To the right of right field, way off in the distance, was the camp office.

"Can you hit the office?" Mack asked.

"It's gotta be two hundred and fifty feet away!" Andre answered, incredulous. "And it's made of glass!"

"Well, if you can't hit it …" Mack said.

"I didn't say that!"

"It's okay if you can't do it. I mean, I bet Deets could've when he was eleven."

"Are you saying I'm not as good as Jeffrey Dietrich?"

"No, no, I wouldn't—"

"Because I'll show you! If you need to see it, I'll show you."

When Andre went up a couple of batters later, he watched the first ball pass to gauge its speed, then got way out in front of the next one, smacking it hard and foul but too low. It went only about fifty feet before landing on the grass, bouncing a couple of times, and rolling to a stop.

"Straighten it out, Andre!" Laker yelled from the sidelines.

But Andre had no intention.

Next pitch: *crack!* This time he got all of it, launching the ball high in the air. And foul. Way, way foul. There was no way it was going to turn into a run, but everyone on the field stared at the ball in awe as it flew. The pitcher twisted his neck so hard to follow it he nearly gave himself whiplash.

"Whoa!" he said.

For a second or two, the ball seemed like it would never come down, but then it did … and hit the side of the office with a crunch. No glass broke, but it sure seemed like it might've cracked a little bit.

The first baseman turned around and shouted to the second baseman, "He hit the office!"

"I know! I saw it!" said the second baseman.

"No one's ever hit the office!" the catcher told Andre excitedly. "Some counselors had a contest last summer to see who could do it first, and no one got close."

Andre grinned. Maybe this *could* be fun.

"Okay, fellas," the umpire cut in, tossing a fresh ball back to the pitcher. (It was going to take a while to get the other one back.) "Play ball."

The pitcher walked Andre on four straight pitches after that, but Nelson was next up and immediately hit into a force-out at second to end the inning and the game, thanks to the mercy rule.

Final score: Camp Roundrock 15, Camp Average 0.

Not exactly the score from Mack's dream but not too far off.

CHAPTER 11

"A MUCH EASIER JOB THAN BUILDING ROME"

The next morning brought a rainstorm as ugly as the junior baseball team's scorecard. At breakfast in the mess hall, news of the humiliating loss traveled swiftly from table to table.

"Is it true you guys fouled off a ball so badly you destroyed camp property?" one kid asked Andre.

"Well," Andre said, blushing, "'destroyed' is a strong word, but yeah, pretty much."

The baseball team wasn't the only one to start play the day before, and the others in action had done their part to ruin Winston's day as well.

"The basketball team got doubled!" one kid whispered to them. "It looked like a layup line out there!"

"That's nothing!" another chimed in. "I heard that the soccer team scored five times … on themselves!"

After a while it became hard to separate fact from

exaggeration, but one thing was clear: all three junior teams had lost—and lost by a lot.

As counselors started moving around the mess hall to quell the talking, Mack turned back to his cabinmates and leaned over his buckwheat pancakes.

"The plan is working perfectly!" he whispered, careful to keep his voice low enough that Laker and Brian, seated at the end of the table, couldn't hear him. "A few more results like this and Winston will have to give up."

"Speaking of Winston," Miles said, "where is he? I didn't even see him at dinner last night."

"A kid from cabin 3 said he was standing next to Winston when he heard about our scores. The kid said he broke his cell phone in half!" Pat told the group. "I mean, it could've just been a stick or something. But he was *mad*."

"That's good, right?" Wi-Fi asked.

"Of course it's good!" Mack said. "First, he gets angry, and then—"

Mack stopped dead as the faces of the kids opposite him were bathed in light from the opening door. He turned to see Winston striding in, his hair slicked back and shirt soaked from the rain. Far from angry, he had a huge ear-to-ear smile on his face.

Winston walked up to the front of the room, cleared

his throat, and called for junior-camper attention.

"So I heard we had some rough outings yesterday as our teams started playing real games," he said, warming up. "And let me tell you—I'm not worried one bit!"

"Really?!" a kid near the front asked, surprised.

"Yes, really! First of all, every team loses." Winston was almost laughing now while he paced back and forth, his wet shoes squeaking with every step. "Michael Jordan lost sometimes. Wayne Gretzky lost sometimes. Even Jeffrey Dietrich lost sometimes! So a loss here and there is just part of playing."

Then he stopped dead and squared his shoulders to his audience, holding one finger in the air as if he were testing to see which way the wind was blowing.

"The key is to learn from your losses! And hey, wow, we've already got a lot to learn from," Winston said. "It looks like it's going to take a little time, but we'll get there!"

Mack shot a worried glance at Andre as several of the mini and senior camp counselors hustled their charges out of the room. He'd expected defeat from their camp director, but this was looking more like frenzied resolve.

"I mean," Winston added, leaning down to the camper closest to him, "do you think Rome was built in a day?"

"Well, I've never really thought about it—" the kid

began, but Winston cut him off.

"The answer's no! Rome was *not* built in a day. I looked it up. Over a million days and counting! They're *still* building that place—just like we're going to continue building our skills."

Mack could feel the desperation in the room as several kids from other tables turned their heads to look at him.

This is going to be harder than I thought, he gulped.

"And the good thing—no, the *best* thing—is that turning you into athletes is a much easier job than building Rome," Winston declared. "Does anyone want to know how we're going to do it?"

Mack could see where this was going. He just hoped no one would take the bait.

But Miles quickly raised his hand. A lifetime of knowing the right answer had trained him to always offer it if given the chance.

"Yes, Miles," Winston said.

"Practice," Miles offered.

"Ding, ding, ding! We have a winner!" the junior-camp director shouted. "'Practice' is the right answer. Come to think of it, 'practice' is *always* the right answer."

Winston then laid out his four-point plan:

Point #1: Junior-camp wake-up time was going to be moved a half hour earlier, to 7:00 a.m., with breakfast served at 7:30 to eliminate some wasted lounging time. Under the new plan, mornings were for general body training, while afternoons were for skills building.

Point #2: To make sure everyone had energy for the earlier starts, all evening activities would be canceled until further notice.

Point #3: Lunches were now "working-out lunches," with simple bagged meals served at the baseball field and basketball court and pool. That would cut several minutes of downtime out of each day.

Then came the mother of all twists.

Point #4: From that moment on, each win on the field of play would earn the members of the victorious team an afternoon activity of their choosing. Everything was on the table for those, Winston told them, even "previously forbidden things like *water sports* and *rocketry*."

Mack didn't need to look around to know the effect this announcement was having. He simply had to listen to the swishing sound of polyester shorts on plastic as half the campers shifted in their seats to shoot icy stares at him. He knew it was a ploy—and not a great one, given that hundreds of hours of mindless toil would go into a single afternoon of free time in the unlikely event that a Camp Average team was able to beat another camp at any sport—but he had to admit, it sounded pretty good right about now.

Not that he was thinking of giving in—not by a long shot. He couldn't help noticing that the two activities Winston had mentioned were the exact ones he and Miles had asked about during the camp director's introduction speech.

Did Winston know for sure that the boys of cabin 10 were behind the embarrassing camp-wide losing streak? Mack didn't care. His face hardened and his jaw clenched as he stared into space. This had just gotten personal.

CHAPTER
12

"ARE YOU STILL RUNNING?!"

Once breakfast was finished, Mack and the rest of the baseball team started to head for the field house, where all campers usually waited out bad weather. But Laker cut them off and redirected them to the field. By the time they'd collected their gloves and arrived at the backstop, their shirts and shorts were already heavy from the rain.

Winston followed them there, had a brief conversation with Laker off to the side of the field, and then hopped into a white golf cart that was waiting by the office. No one knew where he'd gotten the cart from, but it clearly belonged to him—it had a personalized license plate that read "WNER."

"If that stands for 'wiener,' then I applaud the honesty," Pat said, holding his glove over his head like a tiny umbrella.

"I think it might be 'whiner,'" Mack chimed in.

"No, it's an acronym," Sanjay offered. "'Will Never

Earn Respect.'"

Winston stopped the chatter by raising his megaphone to address the baseball team. "You've heard that practice makes perfect!" he bellowed. "But that's only half of it! Winning practice makes winners!"

He hit the gas, and the little cart kicked up a few pebbles as it whirred off. Laker watched him drive out of sight, then turned to his team with a somber look on his face.

"Okay," he said flatly as the rain continued to fall, "so Winston wants us to go for a jog around the field."

"For how long?" Mack asked.

Laker paused, embarrassed. "He didn't say. But he'll tell us when we can stop."

"Why?" Andre said. "We're running literally all day long."

"He thinks our performance yesterday indicates that we don't have the stamina to stick with other camps."

"Or he's sticking it to us," Pat said under his breath.

The coach ignored the comment and instead started to jog. He ran slowly down the right-field line and his players fell in behind him, their feet squishing on the soggy ground. They ran in silence for several minutes. Soon, they passed the backstop and turned up the right-field line again.

Then they passed it again.

And again.

A half hour into the jog, the rain had stopped and the sun was peeking out through the clouds. The boys were on the far side of the field, running past the back row of cabins, when they saw Winston pull up to the baseball field in his golf cart.

But instead of telling them to take a water break and get to drills, he simply yelled another of his favorite new sayings into his megaphone: "Before you can go on a run of victories, you have to go on a run of running!"

Then he drove off again, leaving them to turn left after they reached the backstop and continue running.

A few minutes later, Mack and Andre watched in envy as a group of mini campers and their counselors walked by the office in swim trunks with beach towels slung over their necks, headed for the lake.

Another few minutes later, a yellow bus pulled up to meet a large group of senior campers.

"Where are you guys going?" Mack asked when they passed by, simultaneously wanting and not wanting to know the answer.

"Six Flags!" yelled a senior camper in a bucket hat and tank top. "Unlimited ride tickets—and we're staying over! It's gonna be off the hook!"

After what seemed like an hour, Winston pulled back up, climbed out of the golf cart, and intercepted them at home plate.

"Are you still running?!" he asked, a grin on his face. "Sorry about that. But, hey, whatever doesn't kill you, am I right?"

Soaked in sweat and gasping for air, the exhausted players and their ragged coach didn't even look at him as they flopped down on the grass and reached for their water bottles. But they'd barely taken a sip when Winston called into the megaphone, "Okay, break's over! Who's ready to field some grounders?"

Laker required more recovery time than his eleven- and twelve-year-old players, so Winston offered to lead the drill. He got everyone to line up at the shortstop position, then shouted out the proper way to field a grounder.

"Get in front of the path of the ball, bend your knees, and keep your glove down … unless you want to be *up* to your ears in errors," he said, then cleared his throat loudly.

But once the drill started, perfect form didn't exactly factor in.

Pat was first in line. Winston tossed the ball up to himself and hit it with a sharp aluminum bing … ten feet wide of the waiting fielder. Pat ran after it into the outfield, but Winston didn't wait for him to throw it back. He grabbed another ball and smacked it with such velocity it skipped over Mack's glove.

Every grounder he hit to the team was either too hard or too wide or both, meaning he was either really bad at hitting or really good at tormenting the players—and the grin on his face said it was the latter. Even Andre ended up chasing most of the ones hit to him, and after fifteen minutes, only a few balls had been fielded cleanly.

By the time Laker returned in a fresh shirt to lead some hitting drills, the players' legs were noodles.

From the seat of his cart, Winston watched the weary trio of Tony, Jayden, and Nelson swing weakly at a milk crate's worth of balls. Then he drank a full fluorescent-orange sports drink in a couple of swigs before driving away.

"Remember," he yelled gleefully into his megaphone as he whirred off, "a practice a day keeps the doctor away!"

From the sounds of things at dinner that night, the other teams' practices were no more fun than the baseball team's.

But with each desperate-sounding kid who came to suggest an alternative course of action or ask for a new plan, Mack improvised an answer.

Like: "We're used to losing, and he's not. Imagine how hard this is on *him*."

Or: "If we break now, he'll never change course. If we stay strong, he's gotta try something else."

Or: "*You* saw Winston at breakfast. He's already starting to crack! And no team has played more than one game yet!"

But to his surprise, Andre—one of his best friends in the world—was the hardest to convince of all.

"Everyone's being punished because of what *we* decided," Andre said in a hushed voice after lights-out.

"Everyone was already being punished!" Mack answered loudly. Then in a quieter tone, he added: "We're doing this to put a *stop* to the punishment."

"I get that, and it seemed like a good idea at the time, but it didn't work. Why don't we just give his way a try?"

Mack knew some kids weren't happy with his plan, and he had already begun thinking up ways to fix that. But he refused to give in so easily to someone who didn't seem to care about their feelings at all.

"We always knew this was going to take longer than one game," he insisted. "Maybe two or three will do it."

"But that's just the thing. This tournament is only four games long. Why don't we just give it a shot for the three games left and then enjoy the rest of the summer?"

"Because there's no way he gives us back our summer after that. Either he sets up some other games and forces us to continue practicing all day, or he farms us out to other teams. Best-case scenario, we win one random game and get a single afternoon to do what we actually want. That's not good enough for me."

Andre was silent.

"Do you think the results would have been all that much different if we'd tried yesterday?" Mack pressed on. "We still would've lost, and he'd still be making us run."

"Maybe, but at least we'd feel good about trying," Andre said.

"I wouldn't," Mack said. "Not if it meant Winston got to feel good, too."

Mack waited for a while, but he got no reply. He fished a flashlight from under his pillow and shone it down on Andre, who was facing away from him.

"He's trying to take away our *summer*, Andre. That's unforgiveable. It's uncon … unconsh …" he stammered. Then in a whisper yell: "DICTIONARY!"

Miles, lying on top of his covers and reading a base-ball strategy book, casually flipped a page and said,

"Unconscionable."

"Yeah, unconscionable," Mack continued. "Cruel and unusual. And I won't stand for it."

Finally, Andre rolled onto his back so he could look Mack in the eye.

"Fine, fine, okay!" he said. "I'm still in. But ..."

"But what?" Mack asked, frowning.

"I just hope you're right."

Mack flicked off his flashlight, put it away, and rested his head on his pillow.

Me, too, he thought.

Mack bolted awake. He was in a canoe on the lake, and it was the middle of the day. The sun was right overhead, and he could feel the sunscreen globbed on thick in a line down his nose. He didn't know how he'd arrived there, but he thought, *Who cares?!* He tipped himself out of the canoe and into the water.

Mack swam to the floating dock and pulled himself onto it. He stood and looked out over the calm, glinting water and smiled the smile of freedom. In the distance, he could see the beach of Camp Clearwater, the girls' camp on the other side of Oak Lake. But like his beach, it was empty.

Not that Mack minded. He was just happy to be on the water. *This* is what he'd been missing during all those days stuck in endless baseball practices soundtracked by their proverb-shouting camp director.

Right, he thought. *Winston.*

How would Winston like it if he found Mack swimming unattended instead of laying down bunts or throwing long toss or running for an hour straight around the field?

Oh well, he thought. *Might as well enjoy it.*

Then something strange happened. The water started to ripple and roll beneath him.

Mack put out his hands for balance as the dock rocked up and down and side to side. At first he thought it was sinking, but then he realized it wasn't the dock—it was the lake.

He dropped to his knees to get a better look. He couldn't believe it, but the water level was dropping *fast*.

He looked to the beach and spotted the culprit: a giant machine with a big black tube jutting down into the water. Beyond it in the trees, he could see movement. A figure wearing red short shorts.

"Hey!" Mack shouted, but it was too late. The dock hit the dry lake bottom with a thud.

That's when he woke up in his bed, lying on his stomach. He lifted his head off the pillow to survey the inside of the cabin.

When he saw that everything was as it should be, he realized he'd been dreaming again. But if it was just a dream, why was his hand wet? Mack looked over the side of his bunk to find his right hand resting in a bowl of water that was sitting on a stack of six plastic bins.

He heard a familiar giggle.

"Very funny, Pat!" he hissed.

Mack shook the water off his hand and pulled it back under the covers. But he had a much harder time shaking the feeling of his dream.

CHAPTER
13

"WE'RE FAMOUS!"

Two days of practice later, it was game time again. For this round, Camp Average was hosting Camp Hortonia on the senior-camp field, a short walk up the hill behind cabin 10. It wasn't the splashy new Roundrock diamond, but it had dugouts, outfield fences, and a set of bleachers—which would be full, since Winston had given all junior campers a break from practice to watch the game.

"Okay, boys," Laker told them as they ate bagged lunches on their practice field before the game, "little bit of a lineup change today. We're going to swap Sanjay and Nelson to get our on-base percentage up earlier in the order, then use Sanjay's power bat in the five-hole to knock some runs home."

The red-eyed coach had stayed up all night watching game film on a tiny TV in the camp office, and he was sure he had Hortonia's hitting tendencies nailed down.

"Mack, they've got a couple of lefties who pull the ball,

98

so we might break out the shift. That means you'll line up closer to first base and a little bit farther back, almost into the outfield. Kevin, you'll come all the way around to play where Mack usually does."

"Cool," Mack said, glassy-eyed.

"You got it, Laker," Kevin agreed.

"Great." Laker continued his speech, happy the messages were getting through. "Pat, make sure you're calling for a variety of pitches from Andre. This team has been mashing fastballs, so get some curves and off-speed stuff in there."

Pat nodded, but the messages *weren't* getting through. The team had devised a plan for moments like this: whenever Laker got deep into strategy they weren't going to use, they all just went to their happy places.

As the coach discussed shifts and off-speed pitches, Mack was out on the lake, carving up the surface with water skis. Pat was putting a whoopee cushion on the seat of Winston's golf cart, and Nelson was sitting in an Adirondack chair a hundred miles away from anyone who wanted anything from him. Even Miles, who usually enjoyed detail-oriented discussions, took the opportunity to daydream himself onto the tarmac at Cape Canaveral, the NASA launch site, where he could watch real rockets take flight.

Ironically, Andre was picturing himself on a baseball

field. Just not the one they were on.

After lunch, they marched up the hill to the main diamond ... and found Camp Hortonia already there. Like the Roundrock campers, the Hortonia boys were wearing uniforms—although their jerseys looked suspiciously like hockey sweaters, their pants could easily fit a couple of inches of pads, and their batting helmets had full face cages.

Meanwhile, the Camp Average players again showed up in their orange shirts and mismatched jogging pants.

Not that they or anyone else seemed to mind. It was bright out and a little breezy, and as the players emerged onto the field to start their warm-up, they were greeted with ear-splitting cheers from the packed bleachers.

"We're famous!" Pat said, waving and blowing kisses to the crowd.

"I guess everybody loves an underdog," Mack offered.

As he stretched, ran in place, and tossed the ball around the infield, Mack noticed that the wind had picked up enough to press his shirt to him when he turned toward home plate. That meant it was heading toward the outfield fences.

Then he caught a glimpse of Winston in the stands, talking to the Hortonia camp director.

Conditions were perfect—perfect for the ultimate

baseball embarrassment.

And we're going to deliver it, Mack thought.

Normally coaches don't use the same starting pitcher two games in a row, but with nobody else who could get the ball across the plate with any consistency, Laker just gave every start to Andre.

As the Camp Average team took the field for the first inning, however, Andre hesitated in the mouth of the dugout.

"I was fine getting shelled at Camp Roundrock in front of people I didn't know," he told Mack as he looked toward the bleachers, "but I have to see these people every day."

"Don't worry. Everyone here already knows how good you are," Mack reassured him. "And all of junior camp knows you'll be pitching badly on purpose."

"But isn't that a bad thing?" Andre pressed on. "If Winston knows we're tanking games, won't that just make him madder?"

"Okay, how about this," Mack said, stroking his chin. "Instead of just throwing across the plate, aim for a tiny location right in the middle of it, belt-high. Try to deliver each pitch to that exact spot. That way, it'll be easy for them to hit, but you can challenge yourself, too. You'll be practicing your accuracy even as you're letting them score runs."

His friend thought for a second. "That'll work," he said finally, and Mack let out a long breath.

Andre had a brief meeting with Pat and took the mound. The two had decided Pat would throw out all kinds of hand gestures to make it look like he was calling pitches, but when Andre was ready, he just opened his catcher's mitt and raised it to belt height.

Andre stared directly into the middle of the pocket.

Here we go, Mack said to himself.

He watched Andre throw a fastball that zoomed past the batter right into Pat's mitt.

"Strike one!" the umpire yelled.

Winston pumped his fist, but the crowd behind him was more muted.

The batter looked a little nervous as Andre prepared to heave the second pitch in there, but it hit the exact spot as the first, and this time he managed to catch a piece of it and send it foul.

The third pitch he knocked back up the middle for a single.

"Shake it off, Andre!" Laker yelled from the edge of the dugout. "You'll get the next one."

Andre didn't get the next one.

Or the one after that.

Or the one after *that*.

The Hortonia batters looked like they were hitting off a pitching machine—and they might as well have been. Every pitch was delivered in the same way to the same spot at the same speed.

After the fourth straight hit to make the score 2–0 with two runners on, Mack called for time, and both he and Pat ran to the mound for a players' conference.

To everyone watching, this looked like a serious strategy conversation, and the players all put their glove hands over their mouths to avoid giving anything away.

"You're doing incredible!" Mack said through the webbing of his glove.

"I've given up two runs and four straight hits," Andre protested. "I've got an earned run average of infinity! What are you talking about?!"

"What are *you* talking about? I haven't moved my mitt once in ten pitches!" Pat chimed in. "Anyone with control like that should be playing in Yankee Stadium!"

"Hey, what are we talking about?" Laker said as he ran out to the mound.

"Uh … mixing it up!" Mack said.

"Good—that's what I was going to say." Then the coach put his hand over his mouth, trying to fit in with his players. "Let's get it!"

Facing the fifth batter, Andre gave up another hit that

cashed in two more runs, but the bottom of the order wasn't nearly as skilled as the top. He got his first out when the sixth Hortonia hitter fouled off a bunt, and then he struck out the next two looking—they were clearly just hoping to eke out walks, but on this day against this pitcher, that just wasn't going to happen.

In the middle of the inning, Laker went to talk to the opposing coach, and Mack delivered the next phase of his plan to his teammates.

"I bought seven ice cream sandwiches before the game, and they're chilling in the commissary as we speak." This immediately drew the attention of everyone on the team. "I'm going to award one each inning to the person who performs best at the task I set."

He paused dramatically.

"Your task this inning is to strike out swinging."

At that moment, the Hortonia pitcher—a short, stocky, thick-legged guy with a broken nose and a black eye—finished his warm-up and began pacing menacingly around the mound.

Mack grabbed a bat and a helmet and left the dugout just as Laker was returning.

"Let me show you how it's done," Mack said to his teammates.

"That's what I like to hear!" Laker said.

If only he knew what he was hearing.

Mack stepped into the batter's box, brought his bat to his shoulder as he got into his stance, and looked up at the pitcher, who was eyeing him like a bull eyes a red cape.

He didn't need the intimidation act. For the moment, Mack was on *his* side. He swung and missed at the first pitch outside. He swung and missed at the second pitch inside. Then he took a wild stab at one that was easily as high as his head. Strike three.

The pitcher pumped his fist madly, no doubt impressed with his ability to throw incredibly deceptive pitches.

Then he waited for his next victim: Nelson.

The baseball newcomer held the bat under his arm and fiddled endlessly with his batting gloves as he left the on-deck circle and approached the plate. He had barely learned how to get a hit—now he had to figure out how to strike out spectacularly.

"Like you can, Nelson!" Laker clapped his hands.

A wide-eyed look of inspiration came over the batter's face. He stepped in and watched four pitches pass as the count went to two balls and two strikes. Now was his time.

Nelson's whole batting stance changed as he waited for the next pitch. He pointed the top of the bat toward the pitcher and waggled it a bit. He bent his knees and rocked back and forth.

Then the pitcher threw.

Nelson coiled and uncoiled himself, swinging the bat low like a golf club and bringing it up high on his follow-through. He let go with his right hand, and the bat's momentum carried it down so the tip landed in the dirt.

"Oooh," the crowd gasped in honor of the gigantic cut.

But Nelson had missed the ball by a good few inches.

"Strike three!" the umpire shouted.

"Aw!" the crowd groaned.

Nelson returned to the dugout and got a series of high fives from his teammates.

"That was epic," Mack told him.

"Where'd you learn to swing like that?" Andre asked.

"Observation," Nelson said matter-of-factly. "Of toys."

Miles cocked an eyebrow.

"I reviewed a series of baseball player figurines last year," Nelson explained. "One of them—I think his name was Barry Bonds?—finished his swing just like that."

Batting third again was Pat, who stepped in with a look on his face that Mack had seen many times before. It was the grin of being in on the joke—a dead giveaway prank face.

Pat watched a couple of pitches pass for balls. The next was a called strike, which made him grimace and turn angrily on the umpire.

"That was outside!" he said.

"Not from where I'm standing," the ump said, clicking a wheel on his small black counting device.

Pat watched a third ball pass in the dirt, and then popped the next pitch foul over the heads of those in the bleachers. Full count.

The prankster fanned weakly at the next pitch outside for the third strike, and his face went beet red.

"Strike three!" yelled the ump, drawing a glare from Pat.

"A little low on style points," Mack said as he greeted his friend at the dugout, "but nice acting job with the ump!"

"Thanks." Pat frowned, but then quickly perked up. "I mean, like I care what that guy thinks is a ball or a strike!"

Everyone looked at Mack expectantly.

"Two great choices. But the ice cream sandwich goes to … Nelson!" Everyone patted the winner on the back. "That was the greatest strikeout I've ever seen."

Over the next several innings, Andre allowed a ton of runs but also recorded a ton of strikeouts while Mack awarded frozen treats for hardest ground-out, highest pop-out, ugliest bunt, and most egregious base-running error (a tricky one because it meant you had to get on base first).

At the top of the sixth, Mack told them they'd be shooting for worst relay throw.

"Well, Nelson's got that one in the bag," Pat teased. But as he left the dugout, he failed to notice Nelson glowering on the bench behind him.

As the Hortonia lead grew from four runs to seven to eleven, Mack was as riveted by the incredible feats of his team as he was by the stands, where Winston was growing more and more inconsolable. Moments from the highlight reel that Mack would never forget:

SECOND INNING

On the field: Sanjay and Kevin bumped heads as they both went for a pop-up. The ball dropped into the dirt, and the batter ended up with an ultra-rare infield double.

In the bleachers: Winston took off his cap and rubbed his forehead vigorously.

FIFTH INNING

On the field: A long line drive bounced between Nelson's legs in right field, and two runners came around to score.

In the bleachers: Winston inched away from the beaming Hortonia director, seemingly trying not to be seen.

SIXTH INNING

On the field: Tony knocked a slow grounder to third and tripped over his own feet coming out of the batter's box.

In the bleachers: Winston angrily stormed off, stepping over a handful of junior campers on the way.

In the bottom of the seventh, Jayden struck out to end both the inning and the game by mercy rule.

"People are going to *study* this scorecard," Miles said, marking a *K* on the line next to Jayden's name.

Final score: 22–0. At home. To a camp that specialized in ball hockey.

"That oughta do it," Mack said as he lingered alone by first base, his teammates and the last of the kids in the bleachers walking away from the field.

"If you mean make Winston madder and more eager to punish you, then you're right," said a low voice behind him. "You nailed it."

CHAPTER 14

"THANKS FOR THE KIND WORDS, I GUESS"

Mack whirled to see a tan senior camper in a blue-and-white hat and red tank top standing behind him on the diamond with his thumbs hooked through the belt loops of his shorts. He was the one from the baseball-throw station on the second day of camp, when this whole ordeal started.

"I don't know what you're talking about," Mack said, reaching into the dugout to grab his glove.

"Come on," the senior camper snorted. "No team with a kid as good as Andre loses 22–0."

"What do you know about it?" Mack said, feeling like he was betraying his friend. "Maybe he's just not that good."

The senior camper scoffed. "Not that good? Look, some people like watching movies or listening to music or making their parents crazy. All I do is play baseball and watch baseball. And I *know* Andre has a better swing and better timing than some of the players in the minor leagues."

"Then maybe he had an off day," Mack said. "It happens."

"Yeah, it does," the senior camper continued. "But it's not happening to a guy who can manage a hundred percent strike percentage. To my knowledge, that's literally never happened—not a single ball thrown over seven innings. Honestly, I can see why you asked him to do it—you gotta find some way to keep him interested in the game—but it was the deadest giveaway in the history of giveaways."

"What is it you think we're giving away?" Mack said, trying to stall. For the first time all summer, he hoped a practice was starting and someone was on the way to drag him off to it.

"You tanked that game," he said. "You deliberately lost it."

"Why would we do that?" Mack said, shifting into fact-finding mode. He knew this guy was on to them, but he didn't know what he planned to do with the information.

"My guess? You want Winston to give up on you so things can go back to the way they were before he got here," the senior camper said. "But I don't think he's the giving-up type."

"You guys friends or something?" Mack asked defiantly.

"How many senior campers do you know who are best buds with a junior-camp director?" The boy smirked. "No, we're not friends. I'm sure I get as bad a vibe off him as you do."

"So you think Andre's great and Winston's not. What do you want from me?"

"I just want you to see what you're doing. You're fighting Winston because he's taking something away from every junior camper," the older boy said. "But so are you."

Mack grimaced. "Yeah? How do you figure?"

"Call it stupid if you want, but people actually care about this tournament. We all like chanting about being number two, but everyone wants to be number one sometime."

"So?"

"So despite your efforts to hide it, this is the best junior baseball team this camp has had in a long time. In my last year of junior, we finished second to Killington, but we weren't half as good as you are. Or as good as you *could* be, I should say."

"Well," Mack said, taking a breath, "thanks for the kind words, I guess. But maybe you're just upset we're going to lose another tournament, and you've overestimated a team that's lost two games by nearly forty runs."

"Yeah, maybe," the senior camper said with a grin. "Last word: I think this plan is more about you—getting what *you* want—than anything else. And Andre is getting caught in the crossfire. You don't have to be his best friend to see how much this is hurting him."

Mack had nothing to say to that. He just bent the end of his glove over and let it flop back straight again.

"See you around, Mack," the boy said as he walked off in the general direction of senior camp. "If you come to your senses, I'm in cabin 20. Just ask for Hassan."

On his way down to the commissary to collect the promised ice cream sandwiches before dinner, Mack took one back slap after another from his fellow junior campers.

"That was amazingly horrible!" one told him.

"They'll need to hose down the field, you guys stunk it up so bad!" said another.

"I think I saw Winston start crying a little bit in the fifth!" said a third.

Mack tried to share their enthusiasm, but he could muster only awkward smiles in return.

Was he doing more harm than good? Was he really as self-centered as the evil camp director they all hated? Worst of all, was he ruining a once-in-a-lifetime opportunity for his best friend?

His only hope was that Winston felt as bad as he did. If that was the case, their plan was working and all this could soon be forgotten. If not, Mack didn't know what he'd do next.

He passed out the ice cream sandwiches, then lined up outside the mess with the rest of his cabin and waited for an opportunity to see which way his camp director was leaning.

"Thanks, Mack," Pat said, tearing into his frozen prize with a big bite as their line started to move. "You ruin a meal as well as you ruin a baseball tournament."

In the dining hall, though, Winston was neither his usual gung-ho self nor as miserable and frustrated as he had appeared in the bleachers. In fact, he wasn't even there.

Mack left his cabinmates to line up for food without him. Because they were hosting the boys from Camp Hortonia, Winston had agreed to let them have pizza night—which was normally Mack's favorite. But tonight he slid into the cabin 10 table without even grabbing a tray, crossed his arms in front of him, and put his head down. Then he felt someone brush by him and perked up his ears just in time to catch a snippet of conversation.

"What do you mean we have to work tonight?" he

heard one counselor ask another.

"I don't know, man. Winston just said we have extra prep for tomorrow. He didn't elaborate."

Mack didn't know what that could mean. But he didn't like the sound of it.

CHAPTER 15

"SAY GOODBYE TO CAMP AVALON"

It was still dark when the air-raid siren screamed through camp like a cross between a million moaning ghosts and the same number of ambulances stuck at their most piercing note.

The boys of cabin 10 sat bolt upright in their beds. The noise was everywhere—in the walls, in the air, between their ears.

"What the … ?" Miles flailed his hands until he found his glasses, putting them on just in time to see Nelson half leap and half roll onto the floor from the bed above him. "What time is it?!"

"It's 4:30 a.m.!" Wi-Fi wailed, holding out his watch.

"Who cares?! This sound is melting my brain!" Pat shouted.

"Make it …" Mike said.

"… stop!" Spike finished.

But as Mack pressed his palms against his ears in a futile effort to shut out the noise, he knew there'd be no such luck. This was why the counselors had been working the night before. And it had something to do with the baseball team. As Hassan said, Winston wasn't the giving-up type.

A few seconds later, Laker and Brian burst into the cabin wearing army fatigues and green berets, shining powerful flashlights in the boys' faces.

"Get up, recruits! Get dressed!"

"*Recruits* ... ?" Miles squinted into the light.

"Get dressed or give me twenty, soldier!" Brian leaned down and yelled in his face.

"Give you twenty *what*?" Miles shrieked.

"Sorry! Sorry, Miles," Brian stammered. "Just get dressed, okay?"

Laker made a face at his fellow counselor.

"I mean ... get dressed *now*!" Brian shouted, standing up and puffing out his chest.

The boys scrambled into T-shirts, shorts, and running shoes and stumbled outside to see that every other junior camper had done the same. It was still dark out, but there was a light drizzle in the warm air, which only promised to get warmer as the day went on. They all faced the center of the field, where a lone figure stood next to a golf cart. He was geared up like Laker, Brian, and the other counselors—only he had an army helmet on his head, a bunch of medals pinned to his shirt … and a megaphone in his hand.

Winston.

With a wave of his hand, the air-raid siren cut out. He raised his megaphone.

"Say goodbye to Camp Avalon," he shouted, "and hello to boot camp!"

Confused murmurs resounded among the half-asleep boys. A camp for boots?

"*Boot* camp!" Winston repeated wildly when he saw the blank stares on the faces of his campers. "Boot *camp*!"

Nothing.

"Like, intense army training that soldiers do before going to war! That's what we're doing today! Which makes me your drill sergeant."

Just more blank stares. The groggy campers finally understood what he meant, but now they didn't get his enthusiasm. They also wondered why he was doing this.

Luckily, Winston was getting to that.

"I watched that baseball game yesterday, and I realized something," he said.

Mack's face went hot with shame. He had the simultaneous feeling of being right about this morning and wrong about every other guess he'd made so far that summer.

"I realized it's not skills you lack," the junior-camp director continued as he paced back and forth in front of the golf cart. "Well, who am I kidding? It's skills, too. But it's also character! We need to build some character! And you know how we're going to do that?"

None of the campers knew. Half of them were barely keeping their eyes open. The others were just waiting for him to get on with it. And all were hot and sticky from the heat and the light rain.

"Nelson! Where's Nelson?" asked Winston, undeterred.

"Sir, over here, sir!" Laker said, fully into character and pointing toward a freaked-out Nelson, eyes wide with terror.

"How are we going to build some character, Nelson?"

His mind a complete blank, the longtime toy tester blurted the first word he could associate with "build."

"Lego?" Nelson said.

"*No*, Nelson! Not *Lego*!" Winston screamed into the megaphone, proving that at least the torment could still go both ways. "The answer is *hard work*! Gut-wrenching, back-breaking toil!"

First, Winston said, they'd have to learn to stand at attention.

"Atten-tion!" he shouted, and a handful of movie buffs, like Wi-Fi, stood straight up. The rest just continued staring.

"Not quick enough!" he yelled. "Five push-ups from everybody!"

Slowly the drowsy kids did five push-ups on the wet grass beneath them and stood back up.

"Now, when I say 'Attention!' you all stand up straight, heads up, hands at your sides," he explained. "Okay ... attention!"

Every kid jumped to attention, except for Miles, who stumbled as he brought his feet together.

"Uh-oh, missed one! Push-ups!"

As the kids got down to the ground, Winston yelled out his command again: "Attention!"

Some kids tried to get the push-ups done as quickly as possible, others stood immediately, and others just looked up, confused.

Winston chuckled into the megaphone. "Just kidding. Finish the push-ups and hop up."

"Good one," Pat muttered sarcastically, brushing off his moist, cut-grass-caked hands on his shorts.

After five more "Attention!" calls and a bunch more push-ups, each kid had it mastered. The junior-camp director then explained that an "At ease!" command meant they could relax with their hands behind their backs.

Winston then told them it was time for a light warm-up jog.

"Just like the last one?" Pat whispered to Mack.

Winston got in his golf cart, honked the squeaky little horn a couple of times, and yelled out, "Follow me, men! No falling too far behind!"

"Thanks a lot, Mack," someone said loudly enough for all to hear, proving that his popularity meter had fallen to a new low.

But Winston was on high alert from who knows how many energy drinks and cups of coffee.

"And no talking!" he bellowed, hitting the accelerator on his golf cart.

All one hundred junior campers followed the cart up the hill, past the pool, across the senior-camp baseball field, and through the woods to the camp's dirt road.

Mack expected Winston to pull a U-turn, but he didn't. He continued on up the lane toward the main road. He picked up speed as he went, forcing the campers to keep pace.

When he reached the road, he still showed no interest in turning back. He pulled onto the wide, damp dirt shoulder and whirred along it, the flummoxed campers hot on his trail. Already this jog was making the one after their first game seem like a walk in the park—which, now that Mack thought of it, it kind of was.

Mack looked left and right at his fellow campers and saw a mixture of angry glares and pleading eyes. He noticed that even the counselors were starting to share awkward glances—they were on this jog, too, and had no idea how far Winston would take it.

A mile down the road, the director abruptly stopped the golf cart, and the campers practically ran into it. He hopped out spryly, ran around to the back of the cart, and pulled a burlap sack off an orange water cooler with a tap at the bottom.

"Important to hydrate!" he said, allowing each of the campers to take a drink.

When they had, he threw the sack over the cooler, leaped back into the cart, and drove on along the shoulder without a word.

For a second, no one moved.

"Uh, move out!" shouted Laker, and reluctantly the campers picked up their feet and followed the golf cart, which was already shrinking in the distance.

It was several more minutes before Winston abruptly whirled around and zoomed past them in the opposite direction, meaning the time had come for them to retrace their steps all the way back to camp. Mack could already feel each one in the bones in his aching feet.

When they finally reached the junior-camp base-ball field, it was six o'clock. The rain had stopped, the sun and temperature were both rising ... and their camp was as unrecognizable as it had been on the day of the MAATs. But this time it looked less like the NFL Scouting Combine and more like the first scene of a war movie.

There was a giant wooden wall with ropes strung over it and a string grid made up to look like barbed wire hanging low over the ground. There were tires for run-ning through and logs for carrying in groups. There were chin-up and push-up stations. And the air-raid siren had been replaced with the sounds of low-flying choppers and faint explosions.

"This is my favorite CD!" Winston told the nearest counselor upon their return.

He then led the campers—or shouted them, at least—through hours of drills, stopping only to give them the occasional drink of water and (reluctantly) small, unsat-isfying meals of the sack-lunch variety.

By dinnertime, the kids were sweaty and covered in dirt, leaves, and grass stains. As Mack crawled under the string grid for what felt like the hundredth time, he looked to his right and saw Andre completing the same fruitless task a few feet away.

Camp Average's star athlete wasn't wincing with exertion like everyone else, but his sunken eyes and open mouth made him look spent—more emotionally than physically. It was the first time Mack had ever seen him like that. Not happy, sad, excited, angry, anxious, or determined—just deflated.

Mack searched for the right whispered words to lift his friend's spirits—maybe make a game even of this and give him hope things might turn around—but he couldn't think of any.

"Sorry, man," he said. "This is my fault."

To Mack's eternal gratitude, Andre wasn't in the mood to rub it in.

"No, man," he replied. "It's Winston's."

"But—" Mack blurted.

"You tried," Andre cut him off. "Just didn't work."

The two crawled on and stood up just as the air-raid siren sounded again, ending whatever remained of the conversation.

"Attention!" Winston shouted as the siren abruptly disappeared.

Despite their exhaustion, all the kids immediately stood straight up with their hands by their sides, just as he'd taught them.

"That's it for today," Winston said, grinning at the dirty, exhausted group in front of him. "Dinner in the mess, then showers and lights-out right after that. Tomorrow, we resume practice. Next tournament game for you baseball players is coming up fast."

CHAPTER
16

"WE'RE GOING SWIMMING"

Even though the boys all fell asleep before lights-out, the next morning came much too fast for junior camp. Out of every bunk came the sounds of cracking joints and groans due to aching muscles.

Pat grimaced as he raised a cupped hand to his ear. "Ah, the sweet sound of character."

"Too …" Spike croaked.

"… soon!" Mike wheezed.

Over baked beans and low-fat turkey sausages in the mess hall, they heard that the basketball and soccer teams were thinking of abandoning Mack's plan. At this point, Winston's offer of a free period as a reward for a win, no matter how unlikely that win might be, sounded a whole lot better than boot camp.

Drained and discouraged, the members of the baseball team trudged to the field and lay down in front of Laker to receive the orders of the day. Their coach couldn't blame them.

"Okay, boys," he began before stopping abruptly, a flush coming over his face as he locked his knees together.

Mack took notice immediately and propped himself up on his elbows.

"Um," Laker said, "I may need to use the bathroom. You men warm up. I'll be right back."

Mack watched with laser focus as the coach awkwardly fast-walked to the office, holding his stomach with both hands the whole way. He slipped through the door and shut it behind him.

"Okay, let's go," Mack said, scrambling to his feet as soon as Laker was out of sight.

"Go where? The outfield?" Pat asked, rolling over onto his stomach.

"No," Mack answered. "The beach."

He turned away from the field and walked at a steady clip toward the waterfront.

The baked beans they'd been served that morning happened to be Laker's kryptonite. If past run-ins were any indication, the boys would have fifteen minutes before their coach was upright again and back on the field. That was just enough time to right a horrible wrong—if, that is, the rest of the team still trusted Mack enough to come along.

He walked on alone for a few seconds before he heard

a small stampede of footsteps behind him, and he took a grateful breath. When the members of the team reached his side, he simply said, "We're going swimming."

"But what about Winston?" Miles asked nervously.

"Camp directors meet in Simon's cabin every day after breakfast," Mack answered. "He'll be busy for at least half an hour."

They arrived at the waterfront area, and Mack strolled boldly into the small red building that acted as both life-guard station and equipment shed. In there, he found the on-duty lifeguard, Jama.

"Whoa, whoa, whoa!" the lifeguard said. "What's this? I'm not supposed to have anybody here this morning."

In truth, Jama had had a lot of free blocks since the junior campers were barred from water sports. At first he'd enjoyed the quiet, but then he'd just gotten bored.

"Laker sent us down for a cool-off," Mack said confi-dently. "Just ten minutes and then back up. He felt bad seeing us at boot camp yesterday. Thought he'd cut us a break on the down-low."

"Yeah, well, I think a lot of us felt the same," said Jama, but he caught himself when he saw Mack's eyes widen. "I mean, uh, nothing against Winston or anything. You guys just looked like you were working hard. But ..."

"But what?" Mack asked.

"Where *is* Laker? You're not supposed to come down here unsupervised. And you know I need advance notice of everyone going in the water."

"He had to use the bathroom," Mack said, pleased that at least one part of his story was true. "He said it'd be cool."

Time was running out. It was now or never as the baseball team waited for Jama's reply.

"I'll probably regret this, but … fine. Just put on life jackets and let me count you as you go by. I'll be watching you like a hawk, and you'll be getting out in *five* minutes—no more."

Mack broke into a huge grin. He pulled a red-and-blue life jacket on over his T-shirt, kicked off his cleats and socks, and raced down the hill and onto the dock, which protruded a good thirty feet into the lake. He ran straight off the end and splashed down into the water. The life jacket kept his head from going under, but it didn't matter—after boot camp, even dipping his toes in the water would've felt like the greatest swim of his life. He floated on his back and looked up at the sky as churning water all around let him know everyone else had joined him in the lake.

Within seconds, Tony and Jayden were hopping back out to engage in a cannonball competition. Pat started stalking his teammates like a great white, humming the *Jaws* theme. Sanjay, Kevin, and Reilly scattered, while

Nelson clung cautiously to the dock. Miles simply treaded water and sliced his hand into the surface of the lake over and over, looking for the perfect angle to maximize splashing distance should Pat come anywhere near him.

And Andre …

"Wait," Mack said. "Where's Andre?"

They all looked around. He wasn't in the water, and his stuff wasn't by the lifeguard station along with everyone else's.

"He didn't come down with you," Jama called from the beach. "And by the way—time's up! Everybody out!"

Mack and the rest of the boys thanked the lifeguard as they pulled socks and cleats onto their sopping feet and bolted back up the hill. They didn't cross paths with a single camp employee, and if anyone saw them from a window, they didn't say anything about it later. The boys arrived back at the diamond and found it in exactly the state they'd left it—equipment lying all over the field, Andre on his back, no Laker in sight.

"You missed an epic mission, man," Pat told Andre as he flopped down beside him to adjust his footwear.

But Andre just lay there, his head resting on his baseball glove. Even when droplets of water from Pat's socks sprayed all over his shirt, he didn't move a muscle.

"You okay, Andre?" Mack asked. "We thought you

were with us when we left. The water felt great."

"Sorry I missed it," Andre said quietly.

Mack opened his mouth to continue pressing, but just then Laker burst out of the office and ran over to the field, a piece of toilet paper stuck to the bottom of his cleats.

"Sorry that took so—*what happened to you*?" the coach asked, looking confused. "You're soaking wet!"

"Working hard!" Pat leaped up and started running on the spot. "Gotta beat Killington in a couple days." Then he turned to Mack. "Right, Captain?"

"Yeah!" Mack said, flopping onto his back and bicycling his legs in the air.

The rest of the team followed suit with noodly-arm jumping jacks, one-foot 360-degree spins, and a variety of other improvised exercises.

Everyone but Andre, who continued to lie on the ground.

"Oh," Laker said.

He looked from the furiously moving teammates to their immobile star player. Mack could tell that Laker knew they were lying. But he said nothing else about it.

"Okay," he said lifelessly. He held out a hand for Andre and pulled him up off the grass. "Winston will be around soon. Let's ... uh, let's get it."

CHAPTER
17

"NICE EFFORT"

Over the next day and a half, Mack started likening Camp Average to a landlocked version of the Bermuda Triangle. His life existed in the space between three points: his cabin, the mess hall, and home plate of the junior-camp baseball field. And there was no way out—except to play actual games, which by this point was the absolute last thing he and his teammates wanted to do.

And so when they got off the bus at Camp Killington for game three of the tournament, it was with all the energy of a group of convicts arriving at a maximum-security prison to start their life sentences.

Not that the Killington campus had anything in common with jail, aside from the chain-link fence. In fact, Killington didn't even look that much like a summer camp. The place felt like a cross between a country club and a major league spring training facility. On one side of the grounds, there were croquet pitches, saunas, five-star dining rooms, and pop-up juice bars. On the other, multiple state-of-the-art baseball fields with tall light stanchions for night games … and pretty much nothing else.

Unlike the other camps they'd traveled to, Killington had no field house, no archery range, not even a beat-up basketball court. Its campers were here for one of only two things—luxury or baseball—and it showed.

The Camp Average boys trudged to field six—not Killington's best but still professionally maintained, with short-cropped bright green grass, an orange dirt infield, and blinding white lines—and joylessly went through the motions.

After the outfielders warmed up their arms and the infielders took some soft grounders from Laker, they all took their seats in the dugout. Then their coach revealed the lineup. "Same as last game," he mumbled, forgoing a pep talk.

As Mack waited for the Killington pitcher to finish his warm-up, he looked over at Andre, who might as well have been sitting through a school assembly about the need for good hygiene. Since the baseball team's spontaneous swim session, the normally energetic Andre had uttered just two words—"thank" and "you"—and both were said only when he was served food in the mess hall.

Mack wanted to ask his friend how he was doing,

but the answer was written all over his dull, tired-looking face. Even worse? That look was catching. By the time the umpire beckoned for the first Camp Average batter, pretty much everyone else on the team had it, too—even the coach.

Mack grabbed a bat and a helmet and dragged his unwilling feet toward the plate. For this game, there would be no prizes for embarrassing plays. No effort made to lose in memorable fashion. Just a yearning to get back on the bus and head back to their own camp.

This was the last matchup of the round robin. Since it was only a four-team tournament, every team made the playoffs. But that meant that the boys would have to endure just two more sure losses, including the one today, before the tournament's merciful end, which couldn't come fast enough.

"Touch green, Mack," Laker mumbled, standing way back of first base.

Only then did Mack notice how quiet it was on the field. He looked over at the opponents' dugout, which—despite the four knee-bouncing, sunflower-seed-chewing players inside it—was as noiseless as his own.

He quickly realized why. Most Camp Average kids came from local areas, making the larger group of campers a collection of smaller groups of friends. But the Killington kids came from all over the country to work with top-flight coaches and stack themselves up against the best in their age group. When they looked up and down the bench, they didn't see pals. They saw measuring sticks.

Mack had a vague sense of awe at their crisp pinstriped uniforms and their robotic efficiency on the baseball field, but the lack of chatter in their dugout proved it: they didn't have everything.

"Batter?" the umpire said, bringing Mack back down to Earth.

Mack finally stepped in, hacked at the first two pitches out of the strike zone to sit at 0–2, and then made contact with the third pitch, sending it along the ground toward the second baseman, who threw him out with precision.

As Mack jogged back to the dugout, the infielders threw the ball around the horn at lightning speed, and the first baseman said sarcastically under his breath, "Nice effort."

If there was a kid with more talent than Andre in this tournament—and Mack and every other Camp Average kid would argue to the death that there wasn't—it was the first baseman. He was the least robotic on his team. He'd earned the right to show the odd hint of arrogance by being clearly the best player of the bunch.

Even if you knew nothing much about baseball, you

knew who he was: Terry Dietrich, nephew of Jeffrey Dietrich, the MLB legend. "Little Deets," they called him on the web when discussing his limitless pro potential. But around here he was just "Deets," the unstoppable second coming of his uncle.

Getting trash-talked by baseball royalty didn't happen every day, but Mack just continued on his way. What was he going to do—argue?

Nelson got a bloop single to left, but Pat and Andre went down just as quickly as Mack had, and Killington hitters exploded for five runs in the bottom half of the inning.

The next two innings went by the same script—with Camp Average players swinging early and often, eking out only a couple of dribbling hits and no runs, and Killington jumping all over any aimless pitch Andre threw in.

But by the fourth inning, Killington's players could see that their opponents weren't really in the game.

So they stopped trying as well.

Less than an hour later, Mack lined a fastball to the shortstop to finish the top of the seventh, and the game ended by mercy rule: 13–0. That put Camp Average's record at 0-3 and Killington's at 2-1. Due to a scheduling conflict earlier in the tournament, the Killington junior team had been unable to make their game with Camp Hortonia, so they sent their seven- and eight-year-old mini campers—who lost by just a single run.

That meant Camp Average would be playing Hortonia, the tournament's only undefeated team, in what Mack knew would be their first and only playoff game.

"Last to bat collects the bats," Laker called as he high-tailed it out of the dugout with the rest of the team.

"Since when?" Mack shouted back, but by then the coach was already halfway to the team bus.

CHAPTER 18

"YOU GUYS DON'T SHAKE HANDS?"

Only Miles remained when Mack reached the dugout. He was putting the finishing touches on his scorecard.

"Not a great outing for Andre," he mused.

"Or anyone else," Mack said. "We're trying to lose, remember?"

"True on the last bit, but not the first part. Nelson led the team with two hits in three at bats," he said. "Outside of when he's trying to earn ice cream sandwiches, it's like he can't *not* make contact with the ball."

"On another team that might be a useful skill," Mack said, trying to end the conversation before he felt worse than he already did.

He unhooked their bat bag from the chain-link fence, slung it over his shoulder, and left the dugout. He and Miles were nearly to the parking lot when the path they were following opened up to a small clearing with a gazebo. Beside it was a certain soon-to-be-world-famous baseball player.

Deets stood in their way with his chest puffed out. He was the same height as Mack and easily twenty pounds of muscle heavier—clearly the "Little" was only in relation to his superstar uncle.

"We missed you in the middle of the infield," the unsmiling first baseman said.

"What's that supposed to mean?" Mack shot back.

"What, you guys don't shake hands?" Deets asked, referring to the post-game tradition of acknowledging the opposing team, which Camp Average had been ignoring altogether. "It figures. Your camp has never done anything in this tournament. Why would shaking hands be any different?"

Mack didn't care what Deets thought, but he still couldn't help himself.

"Hey, we beat you once. The 1951 tournament. Look it up."

"Yeah," Deets laughed. "You keep believing that."

"Hey, what are you trying to—" Mack managed to get out before Miles stepped between him and the Killington player.

"It's not worth it, Mack," Miles said.

"Yeah, *Mack*," Deets chided. "Don't want another *L* on your record. You've got too many already."

As Killington's best player walked away, Miles shoved

Mack toward the Camp Average bus and all the way inside. The doors slammed shut behind them, and they stomped past their teammates to take the two back-row seats.

"Miles! What's the big idea?" Mack flopped down onto the cracking green vinyl. "I was just setting him straight! He tried to say we never won in 1951."

The smaller boy put his white-running-shoe-clad feet up on his own seat, pushed his way to the wall, and bit his lip.

"What is it?" Mack demanded.

Miles popped his head up and scanned the bus to make sure no one else was listening. "Deets is right," he whispered finally.

"What?!" Mack gaped. "How do you know?"

"Have you ever heard the saying, 'There are lies, big lies, and statistics'?"

"No," Mack said.

"Seriously?"

"Yes."

"Well, you've obviously never talked to my *grand-father* ..."

"Miles, focus!" Mack seethed. "What are you talking about?!"

Miles sighed. "I was going to tell you to forget that saying, because in this case the stats are right. And they say Camp Average didn't win the 1951 All-Camp Junior Baseball Tournament."

Mack shook his head. "I don't believe it."

"It's true."

"I … disagree," Mack said obstinately.

"Look." Miles pulled a weathered scorecard from behind the pad of paper on his clipboard. It was for the 1951 all-camp final, and it clearly showed a final score: Killington 7, Camp Avalon 4.

"In the camp director's library, there's a binder with scorecards dating back to the beginning of the tournament," Miles said. "I went looking for this one the other day just so I could see it for myself. But it didn't match Simon's story at all. Camp Average didn't get a homer from Bucky Brisker, and Jimmer Nicholson didn't shut Killington down in the ninth."

"How'd Bucky and Jimmer really do?" Mack asked, scanning the card for their names.

"They never even played," Miles answered.

"What?!"

"Shhh!" Miles shot back urgently. "You want the whole bus to hear this?"

"Maybe Simon and the other camp directors have been telling us the wrong year by mistake," Mack stammered, grasping at any possible explanation. "Maybe they were thinking of the 1952 tournament. Or the 1949 tournament!"

Miles shook his head. "I looked through every score-card in the binder," he said. "Those guys' names never appeared. As far as I can tell, they don't exist."

"So Simon and the others just made them up?" Mack lamented. "Then who's in that picture above the steam table in the mess hall?"

Miles shrugged his shoulders. "Could be anyone."

"Why would they do that?!"

"I've been wondering about that," Miles replied. "Maybe to give us hope? Something that's been done before can be done again. But something that's never been done …"

Miles let the thought hang in the air before continuing. "I mean, I didn't say anything at first because I didn't want to ruin it for you or anyone else."

And just like that, a new plan flashed before Mack's eyes.

They'd caught the camp directors in a lie, and there was no way Winston, Simon, or anyone else would want the truth getting out. For one thing, they'd lose face in front of every kid and every parent who ever went to Camp Average. And for another, they'd lose their best motivational pitch—that anything's possible if the kids just compete as hard as the ones on that

1951 team—just when they were trying to become a more serious sports camp.

If Mack threatened to spill the beans, maybe the junior campers could get their schedules back.

"What are you thinking about?" Miles asked nervously. "I don't like that look on your face."

"Nothing, man." Mack shook his head.

Nothing but saving our summer.

CHAPTER
19

"LAST CARD!"

The next morning, it was pretty easy to split the boys of cabin 10 into two groups: those on the baseball team and everybody else. A piece of paper had arrived alerting them to the fact that barring bad weather, breakfast and dinner for all junior campers would now also be served on the field of play—no doubt a further punishment for the baseball team's continued poor showings. That essentially eliminated hot food from their diets, but the news barely seemed to register.

"Last card!" Wi-Fi shouted to Spike and Mike.

The game of crazy eights between the three non-baseball players had been going on in the middle of the floor for a half hour, and over that time several cards had suspiciously gone missing.

"You're …" said Spike.

"… cheating!" finished his brother.

While Brian roused himself from bed to play referee,

each baseball player and the official statistician spent time on his own. Nelson flipped through a fall video game catalogue he'd finally managed to pry back out of Wi-Fi's fingers, Andre oiled his glove, and Pat bounced a tennis ball off the wall next to Miles's head.

"Can you stop that?" Miles asked.

"Sure thing." Pat stashed the ball in the pocket of his hoodie. "You wouldn't happen to have a medicine ball, would you?"

Miles snorted instead of answering, then returned his attention to the back of the room, where Mack had spent the past several minutes whispering to himself in the mirror.

The cabin's most inquisitive member took a deep breath and sidled up to his friend, who was in the middle of making a silent but vociferous point to himself, sticking a finger in his mirror image's angry face.

"Hey … big guy," Miles said. "How's it, you know, hanging?"

Mack started and flushed. He was so deep in his self-conversation he hadn't realized Miles was there.

"Hanging great," he said curtly. "You need the sink?"

"No, all yours. Just thinking about our conversation from yesterday. Everything … okay?"

"For sure. No complaints. I mean, breakfast practice is

about to start."

Now Miles was sure something was up. Mack would rather eat nails than shag another pop fly.

Just then, the morning bell rang through the loudspeaker inside the cabin, telling them it was time to swing by flag-raising and then meet up with their teams.

Mack took one last hard look in the mirror. "It's go time," he said, making Miles even more nervous.

In ten minutes, the entire baseball team was on the diamond, eating tortillas filled with scrambled eggs and drinking milk out of small cartons. It was a beautiful sunny day.

"Hopefully Winston doesn't show up to ruin it," Pat said, casting a sideways glance at Laker, who pretended not to hear the comment.

As if on cue, they heard the whir of a golf cart. Winston came speeding around the side of the office, stopped next to the field, and leaned over the steering wheel.

Without missing a beat, Mack got up and started walking toward him.

"Mack?" asked Miles, the first to notice.

Everyone turned to look. Even Andre's eyes bugged out as Mack wobbled over to where Winston was parked, breakfast burrito tightly clamped in his fist.

"Mack, I don't think—" Laker said, a desperate tone in

his voice.

"It's fine," Winston cut him off. Then he patted the golf-cart seat next to him. "I always have time for my junior baseball players."

All morning in front of the mirror, Mack had been practicing his speech. First he was going to hit Winston with what they'd learned about the 1951 tournament, leaving Miles out of it to protect the innocent. Then he'd calmly name the price for keeping this news quiet: an immediate return to the way things used to be at Camp Average. If Winston wouldn't oblige, Mack would blab all over camp and burst the last balloon of hope for their athletic chances.

It's not too much to ask to keep everyone dreaming as big as you want them to, he planned to say.

But the closer he got to the man and his golf cart, the more his carefully crafted words of persuasion were drowned out by a familiar voice.

People actually care about this tournament, Hassan had said. *We all like chanting about being number two, but everyone wants to be number one sometime.*

Mack's gut gurgled. He thought back to the first night of camp and Simon's account of the 1951 tournament. To shouting out the familiar lines and watching Andre crouch next to his chair. It wasn't just other people who cared about the tournament—he did, too, even if he didn't want to win the version they were currently playing in. Was he really going to ruin that for everyone who ever went to Camp Average?

No, Mack thought. *No way.* And just like that, his leverage disappeared. So he decided on an alternative course of action: telling the truth. Or at least as much of it as he could without getting himself into more trouble.

He sat down on the passenger side of the cart's bench seat to an audible gasp from the members of his team.

"No eating in the cart," Winston said in a low voice, nodding at Mack's tortilla and smiling an icy smile. "Now let's make this quick, huh?"

Mack braced himself and looked straight ahead as he spoke. "I know I'm just a camper here and you're the junior-camp director, but I don't think the new schedules are working. Kids aren't happy. They want meals in the mess hall. They want evening activities. They want free periods to do what they like."

Mack finally turned his head toward Winston, but the camp director's expression hadn't changed. The smile was frozen on his face.

"I totally understand," Winston soothed. "That's why I said you can earn a free period if you win a game. And you've already had three chances with the baseball team."

"That doesn't seem like a fair deal to me," Mack replied.

"But it's the deal you and your parents signed up for when you gave me the right to make your schedule."

Mack winced. That was the trump card, and he knew it. But he persisted anyway.

"I don't think anyone here knew exactly what they were signing up for—except maybe Nelson, but that's another story. If you want everyone's best effort, I think you should change the rules back to what they were."

"No can do, I'm afraid," Winston said, trying but failing to sound sympathetic. "As you get older, you'll figure out the only way to get great at something is to do it one hundred percent. No, more than that. Maybe one hundred and ten percent. Or one hundred and twenty. Or ..."

"Uh ... sir?" Mack asked.

"Something like one hundred and fifty percent. Point is, playing to have fun isn't enough if you want to make the big leagues—and I learned that the hard way. Now, thanks to my way of doing things, you guys won't have to."

Because you'll have ruined sports for us altogether, Mack thought, but he stopped short of saying it because he knew it'd do no good.

"Okay, well, thanks anyway," Mack said lamely, suddenly wishing he wasn't holding a tortilla.

He got up from his seat and began to walk back to the diamond, where his teammates were trying very hard not to stare.

"Oh, one more thing before you go," Winston called after him. "As far as evening activities go, you and everyone else in junior camp get one tonight."

Mack turned back to Winston, a shocked look on his face. "Really? What is it?"

"Social with the girls from Camp Clearwater. Camp Hortonia will be there, too. Truth be told, I tried to remove you from it—especially considering your matchup with Hortonia in the first round of the playoffs—but I got overruled. Bus leaves at six o'clock for everyone eleven and up. Tell your teammates."

Mack was dumbstruck.

"And don't say I never did anything for you!" Winston shouted as his golf cart whirred off.

CHAPTER
20

"SO WHAT ELSE IS NEW?"

Word traveled fast around junior camp. They were getting a night out across the lake when they hadn't had so much as a campfire sing-along since the baseball tournament started. They even got to ditch practice early to shower and change.

Socials were a staple in previous years, but most junior campers had forgotten about them under Winston's reign. Now that one had been sprung on them, some boys in cabin 10 were excited. Others were terrified.

"Does anyone have a shirt I can wear?" Pat asked in a panic after he'd finished washing off the thick layer of grime that came with another day on the baseball diamond. "All of mine are T-shirts, and none of them have any sleeves."

"They don't smell that great, either," Miles offered, wrinkling his nose.

"Says the guy who doesn't have to squat in the dirt

eight hours a day!" Pat shot back.

Standing next to Miles, Nelson pulled several things from his bin and dropped them on his bed with a crinkly thud.

The boys gathered in a curious pack to discover a rare sight, especially for Camp Average: a stack of six unopened polo shirts in various colors.

"Dude, who did your packing?" Pat asked, picking up a bright green one with a small blue bear emblazoned on the chest. "Calvin Klein?"

"I thought we'd have to dress up for dinner," Nelson said flatly. "Also, that we'd *have* dinner and not just picnic lunches three times a day."

"Well, can I borrow one?" Pat asked.

"I guess." Nelson grabbed a black shirt off the stack and walked to the rear of the cabin to change in private as Pat tore open his package and retreated to his bed.

As he had been for the past couple of days, Andre was silent during this exchange. He'd dressed in jeans and a long-sleeved white shirt and was lying on his bed listening to music when Wi-Fi sat down by his feet.

Wi-Fi asked something, but Andre couldn't hear it.

"Sorry, man," he said, pointing at his headphones and hoping his cabinmate would take the hint.

Wi-Fi nodded like he understood but then spoke

again, this time loud enough for Andre to hear.

"WILL THERE BE GIRLS THERE?"

Andre reluctantly pulled off his headphones and sat up. "Well, it's a girls' camp …"

Wi-Fi waited, staring numbly.

"So, uh … yes," Andre said carefully. "There'll be girls there."

Wi-Fi's face went white. "I was afraid of that," he croaked.

Pat leaned into the conversation. "If you want to fake sick, I know a great trick that involves actual puke."

"That's not faking sick," Miles said from across the room. "That's actually *being* sick."

"That's why it works every time!" Pat retorted.

"Guys, you aren't helping!" Wi-Fi was starting to look like he might not need Pat's trick at all.

"Don't worry about it, man," Andre said, chuckling. "It's not like you *have* to dance or anything. Most of us probably won't. Just stick with us."

"You mean it?!" Wi-Fi brightened.

"Of course," Andre said, sticking out his fist for Wi-Fi to dap.

Up on the bunk above them, Mack smiled to himself. His friend was back, at least for now—though he didn't feel like he deserved to enjoy the moment. Nobody had asked about his failed intervention with Winston, and he didn't know what he'd say if they did.

The Camp Clearwater mess hall was a large, high-ceilinged rectangle with tons of banners, photos, and art projects hanging on the walls. In other words, it was a lot like the one at Camp Average, only it had been decorated for the occasion. Strings of white lights were hung over the doorways and along the walls, and the overhead lights had been turned off. Pulsing pop music, originating from a DJ booth set up in front of the steam tables, blared from speakers in all corners.

As the only girls' camp in the area, Clearwater had a humongous enrollment. So even though there were two boys' camps visiting one girls' camp, the girls still outnumbered the boys two to one. Fittingly, they stood along the two long walls, while the boys from each camp took one short wall apiece.

For the first half hour or so, it seemed more like a social for the counselor chaperones, as they talked and danced in the middle of the floor. But with some goading from those chaperones, boys and girls who knew each other from back home got into the mix and started cautiously moving about the large room.

Still trying to shake off his morning failure, Mack

stood by himself in a dark corner, hoping for as little attention as possible. But it wasn't long before four unwelcome guests closed in on him like a pack of wolves.

"Hey, you're on the Camp Average baseball team, right?" asked a short, stocky boy at the front of the group.

Mack recognized him. It was the pitcher they'd faced in the second game of the tournament—and the one they'd almost certainly be seeing again in the first round of the playoffs.

"Yup," he said, trying to seem as disinterested as possible.

"Some tournament you guys are having," the pitcher continued.

"So what else is new?" Mack said curtly, looking past the boy and his friends. "We're number two, remember?"

But the pitcher was just getting warmed up. "This summer's different, though. You've reached an extra level of awful."

"And that's not even the worst part," said a much bigger kid who Mack recognized as Hortonia's center fielder. "We heard your camp director took away all your floater periods and makes you practice all day long. Which just makes it extra sad that your teams are so terrible."

"Is that true?" the pitcher asked Mack excitedly.

Mack said nothing. This wasn't exactly his favorite subject these days.

"It *is* true!" the pitcher said to his teammates. "So while we're hiking Bears Rock Trail tomorrow, they're going to spend all day preparing to lose to us!"

"Who told you this stuff?" Mack said, popping off the wall and feeling his whole body tense up.

"Your counselors told our counselors," the center fielder said. "Now *everyone's* talking about it."

"Well, *everyone's* wrong," Pat interjected, stepping suddenly in front of Mack with Andre, Miles, Nelson, and the rest of cabin 10 right on his heels.

"What?" said the pitcher.

"Huh?" echoed Mack.

"We've barely been paying attention to baseball because we're focused on *real* challenges. In fact, we went on that Bears Rock trip last week. It was the easiest thing ever … for us." His brash, confident voice drew in a few passersby. "Did it in three hours flat. But I bet you won't even make it to the secret peak."

"What secret peak?" the center fielder asked.

Pat looked dumbfounded. "They don't even know about the secret peak!" he said to Andre, whacking him lightly in the chest with the back of his hand.

"That's … weird?" Andre pulled off his hat to scratch his head.

"Totally!" Pat yelled.

"I bet …" the pitcher said, looking around blankly at his friends, "I bet we can make it there, too!"

"Yeah? What kind of rope do you use? How many carabiners you packing? Equipment is important. Tell 'em, Nelson."

As all eyes turned to the resident YouTube star, a sudden shift came over him: his back straightened and his mouth turned into an easy smile, like someone had pushed the record button on his digital camera and yelled "Action!"

"You're going to need one decent pickax per man," Nelson said, clear-voiced and beaming. "But you guys don't even look like you know your way around toothpicks."

"Exactly! Pickaxes," Pat continued over the chuckles of their growing audience. "You never know when you'll run into a frozen waterfall at that elevation. Plus, some of the cliff faces are black diamond level nine difficulty. But like I said, no sweat for us."

Mack gaped at Pat, who coolly crossed his arms and examined his nails, suddenly bored with the conversation. Never before had Mack heard someone sound so authoritative on any subject. In this moment, even

Miles didn't know as much about rocketry as Pat knew about hiking. Or climbing. Or whatever it was he was talking about.

Meanwhile, the Hortonia boys seemed to shrink a couple of inches each.

"We'll … we'll see about that!" the pitcher said, finally breaking the silence. Then he stepped away and beckoned for his teammates to follow.

"Tell us at the game on Wednesday!" Pat shouted after them.

When the Hortonia boys had walked away, Mack gave Pat the hardest fist bump he'd ever received.

"How did you know about that hike?" Mack asked. "Did you do it last year?"

"Oh, that?" Pat shrugged. "I just said that stuff so they'd stop bugging us."

"Wait." Andre blinked. "Does Bears Rock even *have* a peak?"

"ENCYCLOPEDIA!" Pat yelled.

"No," Miles said, slipping into the middle of the group. "Incidentally, 'black diamond level nine' is neither a hiking nor a climbing term. 'Black diamond' is used to indicate difficult skiing runs, and climbing routes are graded by classes. Class five is the hardest."

"Also incidentally, *you* know that," Pat said, "but

they don't."

Mack stared at Pat in admiration. "Thanks," he said.

"For what?" Pat replied, grinning.

"I hate to break this up," Andre interrupted, looking around the room, "but we may have a problem. Where's Wi-Fi?"

The boys of cabin 10 did a quick head count, and it was true: they were a man down. They split up to circumnavigate the room as quickly as possible, checking every inch of wall in the place. They met on the opposite side of the room, having found nothing.

"He wouldn't have just left," Mack wondered, "would he?"

Andre looked worried. "I don't know. He seemed pretty scared back at camp."

Then they heard someone shouting at them.

"Guys! Hey, guys!"

It was Wi-Fi, but where was his voice coming from? They looked out the windows and into the rafters before finally turning their attention to the center of the room.

"You gotta get out here! This song is awesome!"

Wi-Fi was in the middle of the dance floor, surrounded by a cheering crowd. He had a huge smile on his face as he executed a move that looked like running in place and then morphed into leaping up and down to the beat of the music.

"Guess he's okay," Mack said, and the others nodded.

Three of Wi-Fi's dance partners pulled Nelson, Spike, and Mike onto the floor, and another walked up to Mack and Miles.

"Hey, Nicole!" Miles said to their classmate from back home.

"Hey, Miles. Hey, Mack," she answered. "How's the summer going?"

The boys shrugged their shoulders.

"Yeah, that's kind of what I figured. Saw you talking to those Hortonians. Seemed ... friendly."

"Hey, speaking of friendly ..." Mack perked up, throwing an arm around Pat and Andre's shoulders. "These are our friends Pat and Andre. Pat just saved my life."

Nicole perked up, too, shaking Pat's hand and pulling him closer to her. "Pat! Nice to meet you," she said. "Not to spring anything on you, but this is part of the reason I came over."

Mack and Andre exchanged confused looks.

"Oh, it's no big deal. My friend Makayla wants to dance with you. But she's shy."

Nicole motioned to a blushing girl with dark, curly hair and a yellow dress standing at the edge of the dance floor.

"I'm shy, too!" Pat said.

His friends let out a collective groan.

Pat popped the collar on his borrowed polo shirt, walked over to Makayla, and immediately struck up a conversation. It was too loud for Mack and the boys to hear them, but in a quiet moment between songs, they made out just one snippet: "Yeah, it's a little bit larger than a quarter. And silver, obviously. I can't find it anywhere."

CHAPTER
21

"THEY TOOK A SHORTCUT"

As much fun as Mack and the rest of the baseball team had at the social on Sunday night, they were thrust back into reality with two full days of practice. But at least they could be thankful for two things: Laker had stopped pushing them as hard—except when Winston was around, that is—and the tournament was finally coming to a close. Lose just one more game to Camp Hortonia, and they'd be officially eliminated.

Of course, they didn't know what drudgery awaited them after the final game was over—word was, they were going to either keep running baseball practices every day or be reassigned to other teams that still had games left to play. But they were more than ready to hop on the bus, take their lumps, and then return home to find out.

Hortonia was a flat, overly hot place thanks to all the ball-hockey blacktop set between the usual tall trees and the lakefront. Mack and the rest of the baseball players arrived at exactly 1:30 on Wednesday afternoon, ready to warm up quickly and get the 2:00 p.m. game over with.

But 2:00 came and went as the visitors waited impatiently in their dugout for their opponents to arrive. So did 2:05. And 2:10.

"Are you sure we're in the right place?" Andre asked Laker. "Or that this is the right day? No one met our bus when we got off."

"They have only one field," he answered, checking the tournament schedule he kept in his pocket. "And they're the home team. This is the only place it could be."

At 2:15, a man in a weathered Detroit Red Wings cap and jeans ran onto the field from the direction of the camp office. Laker met him at the pitcher's mound, and the two had a five-minute conversation.

After it was over, Laker approached the dugout as if he'd just seen a ghost.

"They're not coming," he said.

The boys stared back at him, their faces unmoving.

"Hmm?" was all Mack could muster.

"The entire team went on a hike yesterday, but apparently it didn't go so well. They spent an hour looking for a peak that doesn't exist and then said they needed to finish the trail in under three hours. They took a shortcut through some bushes and got covered in poison ivy. All the baseball players and half the other junior campers are back in their cabins getting slathered in calamine lotion. That's why no one even noticed we'd arrived."

Every member of the Camp Average team slowly turned to Pat.

"What?" he asked, confused.

"They did all that stuff because of what *you* said!" Miles shouted.

"I didn't tell them to run through *poison ivy*! Oh no. That's on them."

Laker shook his head, not wanting to know what his players were talking about.

"So when are we going to play them?" Andre asked.

"And is poison ivy contagious?" Nelson followed up, scratching the back of his neck.

"ENCYCLOPEDIA!" Mack and Pat yelled together.

"No, it's not contagious," Miles said on cue. "By now the rash-causing agents have no doubt been washed off, and you can't catch it from someone else's rash."

The coach inhaled and exhaled dramatically, drawing the attention back to him. But his face remained a blank.

"To answer *your* question, Andre, we're not playing them. There's no time to reschedule the game before their ball-hockey commitments kick in. They have to forfeit."

"Wait, Killington already eliminated Roundrock

in their playoff game yesterday. So that means ..." The wheels were turning in Mack's head.

Laker nodded. "We're in the finals."

Officially this changed nothing. The Camp Average junior baseball players were now scheduled for another game they probably couldn't win in a million years and didn't want to anyway because it would give their evil camp director too much to be happy about.

But unofficially? It changed everything.

By the time the bus arrived back at camp, everyone had heard about their "win." Almost one hundred kids were waiting at the office, and as the bus doors opened to let the baseball team out, they were chanting loudly.

"We're *at least* number two! We're *at least* number two!"

It didn't matter that the matchup was impossible. Or that they'd been actively trying to lose.

The truth was, Camp Average had made the finals only a handful of times since 1951, and this was the first time since Hassan's team did it four years ago.

So like it or not, this was a big deal.

The members of the baseball team tumbled out of the bus and were swarmed by their fellow junior campers.

"You did it!" they yelled.

"Well, we didn't actually *do* much," said a red-cheeked Andre, taking a series of back pats.

"Pat did!" Miles shouted, holding up the blank scorecard as some kind of evidence. "He took them out all by himself."

"*Accidentally!*" Pat yelled desperately as his fellow campers lifted him onto their shoulders. "It's not like I led them into the path of a giant boulder or anything!"

"No, you just poisoned them!" Miles said.

That drew a huge cheer from the crowd.

"That's not true!" Pat whined, trying but failing to squirm free. "Well, it's kind of true, but ... oh, thanks a lot, Miles! This is how reputations get ruined!"

"Poison Pat! Poison Pat! Poison Pat!" the horde chanted, drowning him out. They carried him off to the field, and the rest of the team joined the parade.

Mack was bringing up the rear when someone patted him on the shoulder. It was Hassan.

"Congratulations," said the older boy, matching Mack's pace.

"For what? We didn't actually win anything."

"I think you'll be surprised," Hassan said cryptically, a smirk on his face.

Mack shot him a sideways glance. "What do you mean?"

Hassan craned his neck in the direction of Winston's cabin. "Just a hunch, really. I heard that you tried talking to Winston the other day. I think your next conversation will be much more to your liking."

Mack's eyes widened.

"Just one bit of advice?" Hassan offered.

"What's that?"

"Don't settle too easy."

CHAPTER
22

"WE CAN SKIP THIS PART"

The next morning a counselor came to get Laker before dawn. When he returned an hour later, everyone in the cabin was up. He looked around the room, stopping when he found Mack calmly reading with his back to the door.

"Hey, Mack," Laker said. "Could I talk to you on the porch?"

Mack stared at his book, waiting for the magic word.

"Uh, please?" Laker added.

Mack grinned and climbed down from his bed. "Sure thing."

Laker was sitting on the porch bench on one side of the door when Mack got outside. He took the other bench and waited to hear what his coach had to say.

"Winston wanted me to talk to you—"

"Why me?" Mack interrupted.

"He was, uh," Laker muttered, searching for the right word, "*impressed* with how you handled yourself the other day at practice. And I kind of told him you were the unofficial team captain."

"I can't speak for everyone," Mack said.

There was a tittering inside and a mad scramble. Mack heard scratching, and then a small piece of paper shot out from under the door. He didn't even need to pick it up to see three large words: "YEAH YOU CAN."

Mack read the note without changing his facial expression. He looked up at Laker. "Okay, then," he said straight-faced. "I'm listening."

"Well, Winston … he, uh, is really proud of you," Laker said awkwardly.

"We can skip this part," Mack said.

Laker breathed a sigh of relief. "He really just wants you to do whatever you can to win this tournament," he blurted. "You know, please."

Mack frowned. "We can't beat that team."

"Winston wants you to try. I've spent more time with you than anyone. It's not hard to see you guys haven't been trying."

"Maybe we have, maybe we haven't," Mack replied quickly. "But if we're going to have even a hope of beating Killington, we've got to go all in. Mornings, nights, everything. And for that, we're going to want some con

"... consehhh ... DICTIONARY!"

"Concessions," Miles said through the door.

"Yeah, some concessions. We're going to want some stuff in return."

"Like what?" Laker asked.

"Like our regular schedules back."

"I can't do that!"

On the outside, Mack was calm. On the inside, his heart was racing, and his stomach was in knots. But he wasn't about to give in now. "The baseball team can wait until after the tournament's over, but the rest of junior camp should get theirs back immediately. Like, today. Like, this morning."

"*Mack ...*" Laker protested.

"I'm not done." Mack plowed forward. "We also want meals in the mess hall again. And baseball scores at flag-raising."

"Yes!" Andre shouted from inside the cabin.

"And evening activities. And water sports. And rocketry."

Laker did a double take. "But you *hate* rocketry. *Everyone* knows you hate rocketry."

Mack looked at the cabin door. "Yeah, well, it's not just about me."

Laker rose and pushed his way inside, scattering the

seven campers and one guilty-looking counselor crouching just inside the door. He grabbed a pen and notepad and wrote down the team's demands.

"And one more thing," Mack said as Laker re-emerged onto the porch, firmly shutting the door behind him. "Miles becomes a full member of the team or no deal."

"What?!" eight voices inside the cabin yelled in unison.

Laker was confused. "But he hasn't played all summer."

Mack sat in silence.

"He hasn't even *practiced* all summer."

Mack watched an ant cross the porch floor with what may have been a bit of a low-fat muffin.

"There are only three days until the final!" Laker shouted.

Mack looked up. "Then we'd better get started. Either we do this with all of us, or we do it with none of us. He's already on the roster, and he's as much a part of the team as I am."

"If he plays, who'll keep score?" Laker asked.

"I can do both!" Miles squeaked through the door.

Mack kept his eyes locked on his coach. "Just a hunch," he said calmly, "but I think he can do both."

"Okay, fine," Laker agreed. "No guarantees, but I'll go ask for these … concessions."

The coach got a few steps from the porch before

stopping short.

"Oh, I almost forgot," he said. "Winston thought this might help. If you win, he says he's taking another job. If you lose, he's staying right where he is."

CHAPTER 23

"THAT'S WHAT THE PROS DO"

Any doubts about whether Mack's negotiation had worked out in their favor were answered fifteen minutes later with an announcement over the loudspeaker.

"Attention, junior camp! Please proceed directly to flag-raising. Then to the mess hall—*not* your designated practice area—for breakfast."

A cheer rose out across junior camp.

"I never thought I'd be so grateful for a shot at buckwheat pancakes," Pat said as he opened the door and led the group out.

Mack stopped to tie a shoe, and when he got up, he expected everyone to be gone. But Andre was standing inside the door, holding it open.

"That was really cool what you did for Miles," he said, holding up his hand.

Mack gratefully slapped it, and the two did their patented full-body shrug. "You would've done the same thing. And he would've done it for any of us. Besides ..."

"Besides what?"

"We're going to need all the help we can get."

The corners of Andre's mouth turned up in a cocky grin. "Hey, that's what you have *me* for!"

"Even you can't do this by yourself. That's why we're holding a team-only meeting right after breakfast."

"Where?" Andre asked.

Mack held up his hands. "Where else?"

In the light of day, the field house equipment room was no more comfortable or sweet-smelling than in the night. Tony, Kevin, Sanjay, Jayden, and Reilly—not present for the first meeting—looked particularly confused as they tried to find seats among the lacrosse sticks and hockey masks.

"Nice that you're wasting no time getting back in everybody's *bad* books, Mack," Pat joked, flopping down onto a bag of soccer balls. "Very efficient."

Mack held court in the middle of the room. "Yeah, we probably could have found a comfier place for this meeting."

"Like, literally anywhere," Pat added.

"But it just seemed right to come back to where it all started. And I know things didn't work out quite like I planned—"

"What, you mean you didn't plan on boot camp?" Andre asked.

"Or everyone hating us?" Kevin followed up.

"And especially you?" Miles said.

"Guys!" Mack yelled. "I'm just trying to say we got here. We got what we wanted. Now we can do something else I didn't put in the plan: we can win this tournament."

The nine others in the room erupted in laughter.

"Win this tournament?!" Pat shrieked. "Good one, Mack! And I thought I was the joker in the group."

But Mack stood firm, not even cracking a smile. "I'm serious."

That quieted everyone down again, and they sat up, wondering what planet he was on.

"The way I see it, we have a few things going for us: first, they think we suck," Mack said.

"We *do* suck," Andre offered helpfully.

"Well, sure ... but not as bad as they think. We weren't even trying when we played them, and they'll expect that same team. So that's the element of surprise on our side."

This drew a few reluctant nods, emboldening Mack to carry on.

"Second, Winston had already offered to host the final no matter who was playing in it, so the game's going to be here. Killington gets last bats because they did better than us in the round robin, but it'll be our field and our fans."

Mack looked from Jayden to Pat to Tony. All were nodding now.

"And third, while it may not seem like it, we've learned a lot this summer. We did the opposite of what Laker told us to do, but we know the lessons."

"Like what?" Sanjay asked.

"When most kids our age step up to the plate, they're just hoping to make contact," Mack said. "But in the first two games, we all went up with a goal in mind, looking for a certain pitch, trying to do something specific. That's what the pros do."

"Pro baseball players try to set world records for most consecutive pop-ups?" Nelson asked innocently.

Andre and Pat burst out laughing, and Nelson's face twisted into a scowl.

"No, they're trying to get hits," Mack continued. "But they do it by looking for fastballs or curveballs or whatever to a certain part of the plate, and they try to hit the ball a certain distance and to a certain field. We can do that now if we're smart about it. I mean, Nelson, you had a hard time *not* getting hits, and I know that guys like Andre and Pat can turn it back on."

Pat blushed, scratching the back of his head, and Andre rubbed his chin thoughtfully.

"That's not sounding too crazy, Mack," he said. "But there's still a big difference between having a one-in-a-million shot and actually winning."

"Right. So just this once, we've gotta take a page from Winston's playbook."

Pat stood up, indignant. "I am *not* wearing short shorts!"

"We're going to *practice*, Pat. For real this time. And to help us do that, I called in a new assistant coach."

He walked to the door and opened it, revealing Hassan standing on the other side.

"You guys about done?" he asked. "Time's a-wasting."

CHAPTER 24

"YOU DO YOU, NEW MONEY"

"We're going back to T-ball?"

After some quick introductions, the team followed Hassan back to the field, where they found Laker standing next to a skinny black tee set up at home plate.

"No, Pat," said Laker, looking suddenly rejuvenated. "Hassan and I thought you all could use some quick work refining your swings after … whatever it was you were doing. It's actually a common hitting drill."

"Andre, you're up first," Hassan said. "The rest of you are in the field."

Andre was skeptical about Hassan's involvement right up until he stepped into the box.

"I was watching you at the Hortonia game," Hassan said bluntly. "You need to keep your head still throughout your swing."

"Why?" he asked.

"Just try it," Hassan said, placing a ball on the tee.

Andre got into his batting stance, his feet shoulder-width apart. He started his swinging motion by shifting his weight onto his back foot as usual, but he kept his head level and his eyes on the ball. He then stepped forward, brought his hands around, and made sharp contact with the barrel of the bat, sending the ball over the heads of the waiting outfielders.

"Whoa!" he said.

"Glad you liked that tip," Hassan said, smiling, "because I've got basically nothing else to teach you."

Andre sent several balls to all fields. He hit a hard liner to left that seemed destined to hit the ground and roll a mile, but Miles cut in front of it.

"Mine!" he yelled before the ball settled into his glove.

His teammates' jaws dropped as he tossed the ball casually back into the infield.

"What?" he asked them. "This game is all physics!"

On the next pitch, Andre hit a high pop fly directly at Nelson, who rushed in a few steps, only to have it fall a few feet behind him.

"Nice try, Nelson!" Laker called. "But when judging a ball, always take a step back before taking a step in. That way, you've always got the ball in front of you!"

Hassan made eye contact with Andre and nodded in Nelson's direction. Andre popped another one to the same spot, and this time Nelson stepped backward—only to watch the ball land a few feet in front of him.

"Keep it up!" Laker encouraged him. "Just gotta react after you judge where the ball's going. You'll get it!"

Andre launched yet another ball to the same spot, and this time Nelson got under it. He held his glove up and the ball landed in it … only to roll right back out and onto the ground.

Nelson's face went beet red. He didn't bother to pick up the ball. Instead, he took a running kick at it.

Patrolling right-center field, Mack was closest to him.

"Shake it off, man," he said. "You'll get the next one."

But Nelson wasn't in the mood for more cheerleading. He threw his glove down—"Nice catch!" it blared as it hit the ground—and walked off in frustration.

Laker took a step in Nelson's direction, but Mack waved him off. He chased after his teammate, grabbed him by the shoulder, and spun him around.

Nelson looked ready to blow, an angry tear rolling down his cheek. "What do you want, Mack?"

"I want to know what's up. Why are you bailing?"

"What's *up*? I'll tell you what's up. First you want me to *not* try when it turns out I'm actually good at some of this, and now you want me to be instantly better at the stuff I'm *not* good at. Oh yeah, and everyone's hopes and dreams suddenly seem to be resting on this."

"All that's my fault, and I'm sorry," Mack said. "But we need you."

"You're only saying that because you're stuck with me."

"That's not true. You're one of us, whether you like it or not."

"What do you mean, 'like it or not'?"

"The other night, when those Hortonia goons had me outnumbered, you didn't have to step in to help me, yet there you were. But since then, you've spent more time looking for insults than you have talking to anyone. It's been that way from the day you got here. What have you got against making friends, anyway?"

Nelson turned away, then wiped his eyes with the back of his hand. "You mean ... you guys actually want me around?"

"Of course! Why wouldn't we? Wi-Fi's practically taken to writing you love poems to get you to talk to him."

"I don't know." Nelson blushed. "It's just ... I've basically had a full-time job since I was five, and I've always been more comfortable talking to a camera than to actual people."

"And yet you decided to spend your summer literally stacked on top of seven other guys."

Nelson sniffed. "My parents' idea. And before I decided to come here, I went to an info session for another camp.

The kids there all treated me weird. One of them called me 'New Money,' whatever that means."

"DICTIONARY!" Mack shouted.

"There's no way he can hear us ..." Nelson started to say.

But Miles quickly cupped his hands around the sides of his mouth. "It's an old insult used by people born into wealthy families to belittle the achievements of the newly wealthy!" he yelled across the field. "Mainly it's an indicator of jealousy!"

Nelson beamed.

"Let me guess what camp that was," Mack said. "Killington."

"Yeah. And so when I signed up here, I figured the best bet was to keep to myself until I could get back to normal life, but I kept getting sucked in."

"Well, consider that a life lesson—never do anything based on the opinions of jerks." Mack clapped a hand onto Nelson's shoulder. "We're not like those guys. We've got your back, and that's not changing."

Nelson squinted into the distance for a few seconds. "Okay. Then I guess I've got yours, too."

Mack wrapped his arm around Nelson's neck and led him back to right field.

"Also," he said, "we're definitely calling you New Money from now on. That's the coolest nickname I've ever heard."

Over the next hour, Nelson upped his fielding percentage from zero to about fifty, and the rest of the day saw just about everybody get a turn at bat.

Miles's physics knowledge didn't help him as much at the plate, but he made progress under Laker and Hassan's tutelage, putting the ball in play enough to give him the chance to leg out singles. Mack did his best to outduel Andre, and Nelson proved that he could still make contact whenever he wanted. He launched a series of balls just beyond the infield in all directions.

Hassan was going to suggest a few tweaks to Nelson's unorthodox style, but then he decided against it. If he couldn't explain what made the swing work, he wasn't going to mess with it.

"You do you, New Money," he told a grinning Nelson.

"Attaboy," Laker added, giving him a high five.

As the hitting drills went on, Hassan worked with Pat on providing a good target for his pitchers with his mitt. But when it came time for the catcher's turn at the plate, the dinner bell rang.

"Tomorrow," Hassan said.

"Yeah, sure," Pat said, smiling awkwardly before turning to run toward the mess hall. "Totally."

CHAPTER
25

"I'VE BEEN *TRYING!*"

Mack stared through the dugout doorway to the Camp Average infield. He looked down to find his glove hand resting in his lap. The rest of the players were packing up their stuff, no emotion on their faces.

It was the championship game. And it was over.

"Guys," Mack heard himself say. "Who won?"

Nobody said anything.

"Guys!"

Again, nothing.

Mack looked at the scoreboard, but he couldn't make out any numbers on it. He stood quickly and ran to the opposing team's dugout, where the players were similarly collecting their bats and gloves and batting helmets. Only it was hard to make out any kind of movement at all as they were way too big for the dugout, their backs and butts pressing against the chain-link fence as they moved.

Were they happy? Sad? No, as far as Mack could tell,

they were as emotionless as the Camp Average players.

Then one of them turned to look Mack in the eyes, their faces just a foot apart.

"Nice game," he said.

The player was humongous and somehow familiar, but Mack couldn't tell if he was being sarcastic. But then he heard another voice. "Hey," it said. "Hey, Mack."

"Who said that?" He turned and saw no one. Suddenly he was all alone. The stands and dugouts were empty.

"Mack, you awake?"

He woke up to see Pat standing by the side of his bed.

"Pat?" he asked. "What time is it? What's going on? You better not be holding a bowl of water …"

"No, no! I can't sleep. I'm freaking out about tomorrow!"

After three long days of practice and strategy sessions, the day of the game had arrived. The boys had done everything their coaches could think of: they'd hit live pitching and off the tee; they'd played long toss; they'd turned simulated double plays until the motions were as natural to them as walking; they'd gone for runs that put Winston's to shame; they'd even studied Miles's scorecards to see what they could learn about themselves and their opponents.

But still Mack wondered if it was enough. If it could *ever* be enough to beat a team like Killington.

"We're all freaking out, man," he told Pat. "But you'll

be fine."

"No, I won't!"

"Quit joking around, Pat," Andre said from his bunk. "I'm trying to sleep."

"I'm not joking around! I can't hit!"

"What are you talking about?" Mack said. "You've always been one of the best hitters at camp."

"Well, not anymore! Something's wrong!"

Then Mack realized: over the last three days, they'd all taken tons of batting practice ... except Pat. Every time his turn arrived, something came up. If not a meal bell, it was a bathroom break or a missing batting glove or an empty water bottle.

Mack sat up. Pat climbed up next to him.

"All tournament you guys weren't trying, but I was," Pat confessed. "*That* was supposed to be the joke. I thought it'd be hilarious to be the one dude hitting like crazy while everyone else sucked, but it just didn't work. I'm zero-for-the-summer, and I've been *trying!*"

"Why didn't you take batting practice? Hassan or Laker or Andre or I could've helped you work it out," Mack said.

Pat was quiet. "I was embarrassed. And now it's too late."

Then he casually reached over and grabbed the teddy-bear pajamas that had been hanging from the rafters since the first day of camp. "And while we're confessing things, these are mine," he said, using them to blow his nose.

Mack shook his head. "Maybe it's not too late."

As if reading Mack's thoughts, Andre swung his legs to the floor. In the darkness, he started putting on socks and shoes.

Mack climbed down from his bunk and did the same.

"Whoa, what's going on?" Pat asked nervously.

"BP. Top field," Andre answered.

"But it'll be pitch black up there!" Pat protested. "We won't be able to see a thing."

"Wi-Fi?" Mack asked. "A little electrical help?"

Two more feet hit the floor. "You got it," Wi-Fi said.

"But we'll get in trouble!" Pat said. "We can't go up there without a counselor. They'll bar us from even playing in the game!"

"Laker?" Mack said and stood up, his glove on his hand.

"All right," their coach said, groaning. "Let's go."

Once on the field, Wi-Fi found the electrical panel and turned on the infield lights. He then reprogrammed the scoreboard to read, "GO PAT." Laker refused to let Andre throw the night before the final, so he stepped onto the mound himself. He tossed a couple of warm-up pitches to get loose, then waved Pat into the box.

The problem was worse than they'd thought. Pat tentatively waved at pitch after pitch, rarely getting the bat on the ball.

Drawn by the lights, Hassan walked onto the field a few minutes later. He helped Pat focus on just a few things: choking up on the bat, maintaining balance, keeping his back elbow up. Around two in the morning, Pat strung together a few nice swings, and Laker called it.

"Gotta get *some* sleep before this thing," he said.

As they walked back to the cabin, Andre asked, "You feel better, Pat?"

After a few seconds, Pat answered, "Thanks, guys."

But the still-queasy look on his face told Mack something else: "Not even a little bit."

CHAPTER
26

"IT'S ABOUT THE FUTURE"

"How many of you have seen the movie *Miracle*, about the U.S. hockey team that won the Olympics that one time?" Mack asked the nine other members of the baseball team as they lounged on the beds and floor space of cabin 10, which had become their unofficial clubhouse.

It was an hour until game time, and Laker and Hassan were having a coaches' meeting on the front porch. Wi-Fi, Spike, and Mike had left with Brian a few minutes earlier to secure seats in the bleachers alongside the rest of the mini, junior, and senior campers, who'd all had their schedules put on hold.

Mack's question drew nothing but blank stares. "Nobody? Okay, good, so this speech won't be immediately recognizable to you." He slow-walked to a place in the center of the room and cleared his throat. "'Great moments,'" he said dramatically, "'are born from great opportunity.'"

"Boo!" Pat shouted, cutting him off. "Party foul!"

"What party foul?" Mack asked. "And what's a party foul?"

"DICTIONARY!" Nelson yelled before Mack could get to it.

They all turned to Miles, who adjusted his glasses on his face. "I ... don't know that one."

"I guess there really *is* a first time for everything," Mack said, dumbfounded.

Pat stuck the index finger and thumb of his right hand in his mouth and whistled loudly. "People, *please!* Why do I always have to be the grown-up?!" That drew groans and guffaws. "I just meant that you can't steal a pep talk from a movie. It's bad form."

"That's true," Andre said. "Bad vibes."

"Hey," Mack said, shrugging his shoulders, "it's that or nothing."

"Then nothing!" his teammates shouted.

"Okay, fine. I did have a thought this morning, though. Might qualify as a pep talk." He sat down on Miles's bed. The other kids positioned themselves on the floor opposite him. "This thought, it's about the future."

"I like it already," Pat said, hugging his knees to his chest.

"Years from now," Mack said, "most of the kids we're

facing today will be playing professional baseball."

"I don't like it anymore!" Pat complained.

"Will you let me get to my point?!"

"Wait, if they're playing pro baseball, what are we doing?" Jayden asked.

Mack thought for a second. "I don't know, most of us . . . just regular stuff, I guess. Whatever jobs our robot overlords haven't developed the dex . . . dexter . . . DICTIONARY!"

"Dexterity," Miles chimed in.

"Yeah, the jobs that take fine motor skills—they'll need us for some of those. Kevin—"

"Special K," Pat corrected.

"Special K will be a motivational speaker. Miles will probably work at NASA or something."

"What about New Money? He isn't regular now," Pat said, wrapping an arm around Nelson's shoulder.

"We're getting off track here, but his kids will be, like, second-generation YouTube stars, and he'll have a really big lawn to mow."

"Yes!" Nelson pumped his fist.

"What about Andre?" Kevin asked.

"Thanks for bringing me back to my point, Special K," Mack said.

"And thank *you* for using 'Special K,'" said Pat.

"See, Andre will be playing pro ball, too, and he'll

have, like, a .350 average *and* a sub-2.00 ERA."

"That's good," Miles said, nodding at the others to offer his statistical support.

"And whenever he sees the guys we're playing today, he'll remind them about the time he was eleven," said Mack, looking at Andre, "and beat them playing with a bunch of scrubs."

The boys let out a collective cheer and leaped from their sitting positions, jumping in place and bumping into one another. Tony felt so good he lifted Reilly off the floor and held him over his head.

"Now *that's* a pep talk," Pat said, grabbing Andre's forearm with one hand and giving him a bevy of high fives with the other.

"Every pep talk should have robot overlords in it," Miles said, shadowboxing an evil silver machine of his own imagining.

"Let's do this," Nelson added with a mean, determined look on his face. He crammed his fist into the pocket of his glove—"Nice catch!" it blared.

The door kicked open, much as it had on the first day of camp. But this time, Laker's arms weren't laden with bags. Instead, he held a brown cardboard box nearly as wide as the doorway itself.

"Present for you." He dropped the box on the floor.

"Just arrived."

"From who?" Mack asked, raising an eyebrow.

"Winston," Laker said.

Nelson pulled a multi-tool from a survival pack in his bin and neatly sliced through the tape holding the box shut. He deftly lifted the flaps and pulled out a pristine white jersey with black pinstripes.

"Huh, looks a lot like—" Laker began.

"Killington," Andre finished.

"Yeah," the coach said. He shoved his hands in his pockets. "Well, time to suit up."

Mack looked around at the somber faces in the cabin. Nelson put the jersey down on the box.

"No problem, Laker." Mack broke into a smile. "We'll be right out."

Up on the senior-camp field, the Killington players had already finished their warm-up and retreated to the comfort of their dugout. Just as the crowd in the bleachers began to worry that Pat had led his Camp Average teammates into some poison ivy, their heads appeared, bobbing up the hill at a slow jog.

"Here they come!" someone shouted.

"What are they *wearing*?" shouted another.

It hadn't rained in days, and the field was as dry and

hard as concrete. The boys emerged onto it through a cloud of dust in mismatched caps, jogging pants, and their orange camp shirts, the sleeves ripped off. Two pieces of carefully stacked masking tape stretched from shoulder blade to shoulder blade on the back of each shirt. In black Sharpie, they'd each written one word: "AVERAGE."

The crowd screamed their approval as the team claimed the field for its warm-up, but on the way there Mack made a detour to the stands. He stopped a few feet from a fuming Winston, who had Simon on one side and the Killington camp director on the other.

"Thanks for the uniforms," Mack said. "They're nice. Maybe next year's team will want them."

"Yes, well," Winston choked out, "sounds … good. Go get 'em."

"That's the plan," Mack said and ran to join his teammates.

A few minutes later Camp Average was warm, stretched, and ready to play. Since they were technically the away team, they were going up in the top of the first. And thanks to his effort in practice, Mack got to keep his leadoff spot.

AVERAGE!!!

CAMP AVALON LINEUP		
1	MACK	2B
2	SANJAY	3B
3	ANDRE	P
4	NELSON	RF
5	PAT	C
6	TONY	1B
7	MILES	LF
8	REILLY	CF
9	KEVIN	SS

"Okay, guys," Hassan said, kneeling on the ground of the dugout and gathering the players around him. "You all know the plan. We're building a lead early before they know what's hit them, and then we're going to hold it. Miles is in the starting lineup to add to the surprise factor, but Jayden is going to finish the game in left."

"Everybody in!" Mack yelled, holding his hand out in front of him.

"Really?" Andre protested as the rest of the boys put their hands in.

"Yes, really!" Mack persisted, yanking Andre's hand onto the top of the pile. "'Average' on three," he said. "One, two, three …"

"AVERAGE!"

Mack pulled on a helmet and carefully selected a bat from the bag. Then he lifted his foot to take a step toward the waiting batter's box before spinning one hundred and eighty degrees in the mouth of the dugout.

"Hey, Pat," he said, locking eyes with the pale, nervous-looking team jokester. "Can you hold this for me?"

From his pants pocket, Mack produced a coin. No, not just any coin. It was heavy, about an inch and a half across.

A shiny new silver dollar.

"I got it on a road trip with my family last year, and I'd been planning to prank you with it on the last day of camp." Mack held out the coin. "But now just seems like a better time."

Pat stared at it in disbelief. Immediately a little color started to come back into his face. He reached out and delicately took the coin.

"Be careful with that," Mack said. "Don't want to lose it."

Then he left the dugout to a chorus of cheers from the stands.

CHAPTER
27

"STEP IN, BATTER"

As he walked to the plate, Mack repeated the facts in his head. *They think we can't play. They think this is going to be a cakewalk. We can surprise them.*

He stepped up to the batter's box, took a couple of slow practice swings, and sized up the pitcher. He was slim and of medium height with arms that looked too long for his body. He had dark hair that poked out from under his cap and the beginnings of what sure looked like a mustache.

The back of his uniform read "Nava," but Andre had told them his nickname: "Nada." It was the Spanish word for "nothing," or the amount of success most hitters could expect to have against him. He'd come all the way from Texas to work with the coaches at Killington, and he'd won his only game of the tournament—a seven-inning mercy-rule shutout over Camp Roundrock.

Mack shook his head. *They think we can't play. They*

don't know what we can do.

The umpire yelled, "Play ball!" and the game was on.

As Mack dug his feet into the box, he tried the same tactic he'd used in the first game—he smiled, wanting to seem like he knew something Nada didn't.

But this time, the opposing players didn't seem fazed at all. The shortstop blew a bubble, and Nada simply smiled back. Then he took a sign from his catcher, went into his windup, and threw a blazing fastball so far inside that it brushed Mack back from the plate.

"Hey!" he shouted.

"Sorry," Nada called as he held his glove out to receive the ball from the catcher. "That one got away from me."

Nada threw the second pitch, another fastball, on the outer edge of the plate for a called strike.

Okay, that's your game, Mack thought. Nada had thrown inside to push him off the plate so he wouldn't be able to reach the outer edge.

Mack prepared for another fastball on the outer half. When the pitch was delivered, he started his swing—only to realize too late that Nada had thrown a changeup instead. Mack was way out in front of the pitch but slowed his swing just enough to get the bat on the ball, sending it sharply along the ground between the shortstop and third baseman.

What luck! Mack bolted down the first-base line as the shortstop moved to his right and dove into the dirt. He stood up and whipped the ball to first in one motion, beating Mack to the bag by an inch.

"One down!" Killington's coach shouted, and then his players threw the ball around the horn.

Mack stashed his helmet and sat down in the dugout to cheer on Sanjay. Nada immediately tried the same tactic—an inside pitch to keep the batter off the plate. But he came in too far. As Sanjay jumped back, the ball brushed his shirt on the way by.

"Boo!" yelled the Camp Average fans in the stands.

"Take your base!" the ump told Sanjay, directing him to first. Then he offered a warning to Nada. "Once is an accident. Twice in two batters is deliberate. Any more of that, and you're going to watch the rest of the game from the dugout."

But Nada didn't need any more. He'd planted the seed inside the head of every Camp Average batter. Only problem was, it wasn't going to work on Andre—and Killington knew it.

When Andre stepped into the box, Deets called a time-out, and he and the catcher ran to the mound for a conference. They covered their mouths with their gloves as they talked.

"Is that how dumb we look when we do that?" Pat glanced around at his teammates on the dugout bench. "I mean, it's not like we can read lips."

"I can," Miles said matter-of-factly. "Just not through a baseball glove."

When the conference ended, the pitcher turned his focus to the plate and Andre stepped up.

"Guys …" Nelson said back through the chain-link fence from the on-deck circle. "Nada and Andre seem ready. Why is the catcher standing there?"

It was true. The catcher wasn't in his crouch. Instead, he held his left arm parallel to the ground as the pitcher went into his windup. When Nada threw the pitch, it was head-height and two feet wide of the plate.

"Ball!" the umpire shouted.

"Well, *yeah*," said Pat, rolling his eyes.

Andre looked desperately at his dugout.

"Oh no," Mack said.

"What?" Nelson asked.

"They're intentionally walking him. They don't want to give him the chance to go for extra bases with a runner already on."

Three comically off-the-plate balls later, Camp Average had runners at first and second, and it was Nelson's turn at the plate.

"Here we go, New Money!" Laker shouted from his position between first base and the mouth of the Camp Average dugout, where he'd already nervously chomped an entire bag of sunflower seeds, shells and all.

As Nelson walked to the plate, he tried to keep his eyes away from the fielders. He didn't want to see if anyone on the team remembered him, if they recognized his nickname, anything. He also didn't want to look at Nada any more than he had to after the inside pitches he'd thrown at Mack and Sanjay.

So when he got up to the plate, set his feet in the batter's box, and looked up, he was shocked to find two infielders standing what felt like right on top of him. The second baseman and shortstop had stayed in their normal positions, but the first and third basemen had come in about thirty feet each.

What was worse, Nelson noticed the outfielders standing just beyond the bases, in what had become his sweet spot for bloop hits. In fact, the left fielder was standing far enough in he could cover third if Sanjay tried to steal.

"Hey, ump! What's the deal?" Hassan yelled from third base.

The white-haired, round-bellied Killington coach burst out of his team's dugout. "It's a legal defensive setup!" he yelled, waving a beat-up copy of the tournament rulebook.

After quick inspection, the ump agreed with the coach. "Step in, batter," he told Nelson, who obliged with shaky legs.

Nada seemed to stare right through him as he took the signs from his catcher, then reared back and threw a fastball down the middle for a strike. He followed that up with a heater that caught the inside corner for strike two.

Nelson looked paralyzed, and from the bench Mack could see why. If he popped the ball over the bases, it'd be caught for sure. If he hit a soft grounder or line drive to the left or right, it'd be swallowed up by one of the two suffocatingly close defenders.

But he refused to strike out just standing there. On Nada's third pitch, a plunging curveball, Nelson got his bat around and hit the ball along the ground up the middle—and right into Nada's waiting glove.

The pitcher whipped the ball to the shortstop covering second. He beat Andre to the base, then relayed it to the second baseman covering first to get Nelson.

"What just happened?" Nelson asked in a daze.

"Double play," Deets told him. "Thanks, *New Money*."

As the smirking Killington players jogged off the field, the reality of the situation became clear to Mack: these guys were too smart and determined to take anyone lightly. They'd studied the Camp Average players' tendencies and were playing a game they'd scripted in advance.

But one thought still gave him hope: Killington could *pitch* around Andre, but they couldn't *hit* around him.

Camp Average's ace took the mound and promptly struck out the first two batters, digging into his full repertoire of pitches for the first time all summer.

Then it was Deets's turn to bat. Andre had faced him in the round robin, giving up four hits in four at bats, but he might as well have been sleepwalking then. Now the right-handed power hitter seemed bigger, more imposing, and more confident. The bat hung from his hand like an extension of his arm.

As Deets stretched and knocked the dirt off his cleats, he did something Andre didn't remember from the first meeting. Something, in fact, Andre had never seen before at any level. Deets started a conversation.

"Nice curve," he said loudly enough for Andre and pretty much everyone else on the field to hear. "Really froze our boys."

"Uh," Andre said, "thanks?"

"See, I'm guessing that's your usual out pitch," Deets continued. "So if this at bat gets to two strikes, that's what I'll be expecting."

Andre nodded politely, a puzzled look on his face. Should he pitch? Wait for a lull in the discourse?

"But you know, now that I've said that, you're probably not going to throw it anymore. There goes my advantage, I guess. You could throw a fastball or a changeup for the out pitch, or just gun it right into the dirt and make me chase it."

Truthfully, Andre didn't even have an out pitch. He had just been taking each situation as it came and watching Pat's signs.

Finally, Hassan interjected. "Ump, can we just play ball, please?"

"That's enough, batter," the ump said.

Deets mimicked zipping his lips, but he had said more than enough. He seemed to know Andre's repertoire even better than Andre did, and the pitcher was suddenly unsure of what to throw.

Pat put one finger down and tapped his outside leg, calling for a fastball on the outer half of the plate.

Andre paused, then shook his head.

Pat put down three fingers for a changeup.

Again Andre shook him off.

There was only one pitch left in Andre's arsenal: the curveball. If Deets thought that was his out pitch, why not throw it first?

Pat reluctantly put down two fingers, but he tapped his outside leg furiously, wanting the ball nowhere near the plate.

Andre nodded and reflexively positioned his fingers around the ball. He rotated his shoulders, suddenly feeling a bit tight. Deets's talking hadn't just got him thinking too much—it'd also got him out of his rhythm.

Andre reared back and threw the curve. But he missed his spot by almost a foot, putting the ball over the center of the plate.

Clearly waiting on a breaking ball, Deets swung easily and smacked the ball cleanly. It leaped off his bat and headed toward the outfield. Andre whirled to watch it sail several feet over the fence in left-center.

Home run.

Deets dropped his bat and started up the first-base line. Andre expected a few words, but Deets said nothing. He just smiled.

After Deets's slow trot around the bases, Andre got the next batter to pop up to shallow left field to end the inning.

Score after one: 1–0, Killington.

Not exactly the way they'd written it up.

CHAPTER
28

"DO YOUR WORST!"

"Stupid!" Andre slammed his glove down onto the bench. "I threw the pitch he wanted me to throw!"

"Don't worry about it, man," Mack said, patting him on the back. "It's one run. We've still got eight innings."

"Eight innings ... in which I could see him three or four more times!" Andre said. "He's in my head, Mack!"

For once, Mack didn't know what to say. He was rubbing his temples, trying to force his mind into gear, when he heard a voice over his shoulder.

"I've got an idea."

The boys turned to look up at Nelson.

"What idea?" Andre asked him.

"Don't worry. I'll take care of it."

Nelson hustled to the edge of the dugout and scanned the crowd in the stands. He found Brian, got his attention, and waved frantically for him to come over.

Mack and Andre watched as Nelson whispered something to their counselor. Brian looked confused but shrugged his shoulders and took off down the hill.

"Okay," Pat said from the on-deck circle, turning Andre's attention back to the game. He tightened his batting gloves and exhaled loudly. "Here goes nothing."

Before starting the long walk to the plate he looked back at Mack, who pointed at the pants pocket where Pat's silver dollar now safely resided.

"You got *this*," he said.

Pat smiled and narrowed his eyes. Then he nearly skipped to the plate, drawing cheers from the crowd.

"Lotta swagger for a guy who's hit .000 for the tournament," the Killington catcher said under his breath.

Pat quickly turned to look at him, a sympathetic frown on his face. "Hey, man," he said. "I'm really sorry."

"About what?" the catcher asked.

"They didn't tell you?!" Pat looked shocked. "That's just mean."

The catcher gasped. "Tell me wha—"

Pat abruptly pivoted back to the pitcher and stepped into the box. "Okay!" he shouted. "Do your worst!"

The catcher dropped his head, realizing he'd been tricked, but again the crowd shouted its approval for

Pat. He set his feet and tapped the bat on the plate before bringing it up to his shoulder.

"Thank you, batter," the ump said impatiently.

"You're welcome!" Pat replied.

What normally would've earned groans from his teammates only drew more cheering.

"Let's go, Pat!" they yelled. "Give it a ride!"

The first two pitches were low and off the plate. Pat waited patiently for a fastball, suddenly feeling in his element.

The next pitch was to his liking. Pat swung a bit behind it but still made contact, sending it over the first baseman's head for an opposite-field single.

Nada kicked the dirt on the mound, and the right fielder scooped up the ball and threw it to second. As the roars from the Camp Average crowd died down, Laker sidled up to Pat at first base.

"Nice one," he said.

Pat jumped and turned around, nearly stepping off the bag entirely. "Laker?! You scared me! What are you doing here?"

"I'm the first-base coach."

"Since when?"

"Since all tournament. Where did you think I was going while you guys batted every game?"

"I don't know," Pat said. "The bathroom?"

"What do you think Hassan is doing at third base?"

Pat scoffed. "He's third-base coach. Everyone knows that."

The coach closed his eyes hard and pinched the bridge of his nose. "Just try not to get thrown out on the base-paths, huh?"

Nada was still so angry about giving up a hit that his next pitch plunged into the dirt and bounced between the catcher's legs, allowing Pat to advance to second. The pitcher settled down and got Tony to pop out to right, but Pat tagged up and advanced to third. Then it was time for Miles's first at bat of the tournament.

The smallest batting helmet in the Camp Average equipment bag was still oversized for Miles—it looked like it was eating his head as he walked to the plate. And though the Killington players hadn't had any box-score info or video footage to break down on him, they clearly didn't think much of the diminutive scorekeeper.

"Two down!" their shortstop joked, holding up the index and pinkie fingers on his right hand.

Miles stepped into the batter's box and seemed to go through a checklist in his head: set feet shoulder-width apart, rest bat on shoulder, raise back elbow. He then choked up so high on the bat that he came close to holding it by the aluminum barrel.

Nada shook his head in disbelief. He threw a fastball down the middle that Miles barely even looked at.

"Strike!" called the ump.

Miles stood unmoving. Nada threw the second pitch exactly as he had the first, but the result was different. Miles bent his knees and swiveled his whole body toward the pitcher. He moved his left hand down to the end of the bat and squared it over the plate.

The fastball pinged off it, straight down the first-base line. Miles dropped the bat and took off for first while Pat ran for home. The catcher chased the ball and picked it up, but there was no time to get back to the plate before Pat did, so he threw to first instead. As the ump called Miles out, Pat stomped on home plate for Camp Average's first run of the game.

"What just happened?" asked Deets, dumbfounded.

Pat was about to open his mouth, but Miles got there first. "It's called the squeeze play," he said, stopping on his way back to the dugout.

"I know what it's called, Scorekeeper," said Deets, fuming. "I've seen it a million times."

"Yeah, well, thanks for not covering the first-base line."

"Oooooh!" shouted the crowd.

Miles then joined his teammates in the excited mob

outside the dugout, and Deets yanked his cap down to his eyebrows.

"Two down?" the shortstop said again, trying to look on the bright side.

Deets just glared at him.

With the bases clear and the Killington team fuming, Nada mixed a couple of nasty curveballs with a pair of hard fastballs on the corners and struck out Reilly on four pitches.

But the damage had been done.

Score in the middle of the second: 1–1.

CHAPTER
29

"ANY LAST WORDS, MACK?"

In the bottom of the second inning, Andre struck out one and got two to ground out—and suddenly the game was a pitchers' duel. The entire third inning and top of the fourth yielded just one hit—a Killington single—and another intentional walk for Andre. Neither base runner got farther than first.

But Deets was up in the bottom of the fourth.

Andre took a deep, nervous breath as he pulled on his A's cap and grabbed his glove. But when he tried to leave the dugout, a hand clutched him from behind. He turned to see Nelson holding out a pair of earplugs.

"Gross," Andre said.

"Totally," Nelson replied. "But trust me—you won't hear a thing out there."

"That's genius, Nelson!" Mack said, then turned to Andre. "If Deets puts the ball in play, yank them. Otherwise, just leave them in."

Andre looked toward the plate, where the hulking figure was swinging his bat like an ax and talking nonstop to Pat—and he understood. He made a disgusted face, then grabbed the plugs and jammed them in his ears.

Immediately the world went quiet. He looked around at the animated faces of his fellow campers in the stands, but he couldn't hear a word, even when they seemed to be shouting. Everything was as still and calm as if he were alone in a rowboat on a lake on a windless day.

On the mound he watched Deets's lips moving, but Andre couldn't tell whether he was talking to himself or someone else. He couldn't even hear the thwap of the ball as it landed in his glove. He just watched Pat's fingers for the signs and pitched what he called for. Fastball, outside corner: Called strike. Changeup, inner half: Foul tip. Curveball, inside: Ball. Fastball, inside: Ball. Fastball, inside: Swinging strike.

Strikeout.

Deets walked off yelling at the ground, and Andre got the next two batters to pop out and ground out to end the inning. He took out the earplugs as he got back to the dugout, and then he heard it—the crowd was chanting his name.

"Andre! Andre! Andre!"

He looked up at the stands to see that even Winston had joined in the chant.

"How long has that been going on?"

"Only since you struck out Deets." Mack smiled. "Don't worry. They stopped for pitches. They didn't want to distract you."

The fifth, sixth, and seventh innings went by in a blur, with Nada continuing to mow down the Camp Average players in order, apart from Andre's third intentional walk at the start of the seventh.

But the Killington boys were showing signs of figuring Andre out. They had put two runners on in each of the fifth and sixth innings, then loaded the bases in the seventh before Andre got Deets to pop up to deep center field.

Though the score was tied, the fans started to grow uneasy.

"They're getting the bat on the ball!" Mack heard one spectator say to his companion.

"But Andre's not tired! He just has to switch it up, keep them guessing!"

"No, we need some hits!"

But no such luck. After Camp Average went three-up, three-down at the top of the eighth, Killington came out confident in the bottom of the inning. Andre was confident, too, because he was facing the bottom of the order.

He got the first batter to ground out, then gave up a walk and a double to put runners on second and third. After he got the next hitter to pop up to Pat behind the plate, the crowd seemed to think he would find a way to sneak out of this jam as well.

"Let's go, Andre!" they yelled, though Andre had the earplugs in and couldn't hear them.

He stared down the plate as Pat called for a fastball away. But he missed his mark and threw it right down the middle. The hitter smashed the ball down the line in left for a double that could've become an inside-the-park home run if Jayden, who'd replaced Miles in the field, hadn't taken a perfect path to cut it off. Still, both of the other runners crossed the plate.

Score: 3–1, Killington.

Now Andre didn't need the earplugs. The ballpark went silent outside of a few high-fiving hands in the Killington dugout.

He ended the rally by inducing a ground ball to first base, which Tony handled easily.

But Killington had a two-run lead and was suddenly just three outs from victory. Even if Camp Average managed to score two in the ninth—double the number of runs they'd scored in the first eight innings combined—

they'd still be facing the top of the Killington order in the bottom of the inning.

Nelson did the math in his head, then said out loud, "So *this* is why having last bats is a good thing."

The rest of his team turned and stared at him, not having the energy to ask what he was talking about. Even worse, Killington was changing pitchers: the catcher, who had been lightly warming up his arm all game behind the plate, was taking the ball to close things out for his team. Meanwhile, Nada was donning the catcher's gear as his team didn't want to lose his bat in the lineup.

"Any last words, Mack?" Pat asked, exhausted, as the team captain got set to hit first in the inning.

"Ask Killington that." He pulled a bat from the bag. "I'm getting a hit."

As Mack left the dugout, he began whistling. *Whoo, whoo, whoo-whoo. Whoo, whoo, whoo-whoo.*

To the average person, the notes would've sounded random, but to a Camp Average person they were unmistakable.

"We're number two," Andre sang softly. Then louder: "We're number two!"

The rest of the dugout joined in, pounding on the chain-link fence. Then the fans in the nearest part of the stands. Then every fan in the stands. Then every person in a one-mile radius who wasn't either Winston or a camper from Killington. Back in the kitchen, the cooks preparing dinner chanted, too.

"WE'RE NUMBER TWO! WE'RE NUMBER TWO!"

"This doesn't even make sense!" Winston tried but failed to shout above them. "Who wants to be number two?!"

The bat felt weightless in Mack's hands when he stepped into the box to face the new pitcher, who seemed both as confused as Winston and way more intimidated by the noise.

Mack had been paying attention during each of his at bats, and the pitches to him had all gone according to a game plan Killington had set out for him. Because it had worked perfectly on him so far, he was counting on the new pitcher following the same road map.

The first pitch was inside, and Mack made a big show of jumping back.

"Ball!" the umpire called.

The second was on the outside corner, and Mack jumped all over it. He hit the ball sharply back up the middle and past second base. He arrived at first and pointed at his supporters in the stands, who jumped and stomped their feet on the metal bleachers.

With the pitcher shaken by both the noise and the hit, Sanjay managed to get a five-pitch walk. That put Andre at the plate with none out and runners on first and second.

"Will they walk him?" Nelson grabbed a bat to head to the on-deck circle.

"They can't," Pat said. "Can they?"

"That'd load the bases with none out," Miles said. "They *have* to pitch to him."

Both the Killington coach and Deets ran to the mound for a huddle with the pitcher. They didn't need to hold their gloves over their mouths for this one. Everyone on the field and in the stands was having the same conversation.

Andre stood back from the plate taking practice swings. He eyed the three-person conference sixty feet away from him and swung through their image in his mind's eye.

When the pitcher stepped back onto the mound, breathing hard and staring down the backstop, it was clear right away—they were going to pitch to Andre. After all, they'd been avoiding him only on reputation. Maybe they thought he wasn't as good as people said?

He didn't give them time to change their minds, taking a huge cut at the first pitch. The ball screamed off his bat. Had it been a few feet higher, it would've gone out of the park for a home run, but instead it just dented the wall in right-center and ricocheted back onto the field.

Mack headed home, Sanjay ran around second to third, and Andre hustled and slid into second before the throw from the right fielder.

Andre stood and clapped his hands as his fellow campers resumed chanting his name or howled at the sky. Winston grabbed Simon by the shoulders and shook him excitedly while the Killington director covered his ears.

One run in. One more to tie. Two more to take the lead. Next up: Nelson.

The Killington fielders had tried shifting strategy for Andre, but they showed no sign of doing the same for Camp Average's contact hitter. With runners on second and third and none out, the first and third basemen again played in, and the outfielders set up just past the infield as they had for Nelson all game.

He looked out of breath as he watched the defenders shift into place. He appeared to be dreading the moment he'd have to step into the box and surely, to his way of thinking, kill the momentum for his team.

Mack watched Nelson's breath catch in his throat and stepped out of the dugout. "Time!" he called.

"Time!" the plate umpire repeated.

Mack ran up to Nelson and put his hat over his mouth. Nelson did the same with his batting helmet, but his voice just echoed inside it.

"It's useless, Mack. They know what I can do!" he boomed.

"No way. Not a chance," Mack whispered. "What I'm gonna say now is as true today as it was for your first encounter with Killington: these guys don't know a thing about you."

Nelson put the helmet fully over his face and breathed into it for a few seconds. Then he pulled it down again to reveal his eyes.

"So … what should I do?"

Mack paused. "Swing for the fences."

"Excuse me?"

"Wait for your pitch. Then hit the ball as hard as you can."

"That can't be it."

"That's it."

"But what if I get out?"

"Then you get out. Big deal. Just don't go up afraid. Go up trying to hammer it all the way to Camp Clearwater."

The umpire closed in on them. "Wrap it up, fellas. We got a game to play."

Mack nodded at Nelson and ran back to the dugout. Then the worried batter looked up the middle of the infield to Andre at second base, and he nodded, too.

"Big deal," Nelson repeated Mack's words and

slapped his helmet into place, not even bothering to do up the strap.

As soon as he stepped in and got his feet set, the first pitch came barreling down on him. He fouled it off. Then he fouled off the next pitch to go down 0–2. Then he fouled off four more pitches. Inside, outside, high, low—the pitches got farther and farther out of the strike zone.

Then all at once, he let a pitch in the dirt pass. He watched two more pitches way off the plate go by.

"Full count!" the umpire yelled.

Nelson knew the pitcher had a choice to make: either he could continue throwing outside the zone and risk giving him a free pass to first, or he could throw a strike and challenge him.

The pitcher uncorked a sinking fastball, and Nelson swung low with all his might. He hit it cleanly with the barrel of the bat, and the ball leaped away into the sky at a steep angle. No, it wasn't heading out of the park. But it was definitely going over the head of the center fielder, who was essentially playing second base.

"Run!" Laker yelled from first.

Nelson didn't wait to watch the ball. He took off for first, and Laker waved him to second, where he slid in safe. He stood up and surveyed the bases. He was the only one out there. Both Sanjay and Andre had scored.

"That's my guy!" Winston shouted as the crowd howled and whooped. "I *knew* he could do it!"

Nelson's jaw dropped as he turned back toward the dugout, which looked like it was going to burst from all the activity inside it. Andre pushed his way inside as Mack and Miles screamed in his ear and wrapped their arms around him. Pat was so busy jumping in place he almost forgot to leave the on-deck circle.

The new pitcher at last settled down to get Pat, Tony, and Jayden in order, stranding Nelson at second. But Camp Average had taken the lead.

Score after the top of the ninth: 4–3, Camp Average.

CHAPTER
30

"I'M GOOD, COACH"

"How you feeling, Andre?" Laker asked jubilantly. His star pitcher was about to take the field to put away a one-run championship win.

"I'm good, Coach," Andre said. He pulled on his hat and glove and ran to the mound.

Laker beamed. Andre had called him "Coach."

But one problem remained: Camp Average's star pitcher had been throwing all game, and he was just ten pitches from the team limit of eighty-five. He needed to get this inning done fast or else he was coming out.

Andre got off to a good start, forcing the leadoff batter into a groundout on two pitches. Then he threw two more and got the second hitter to pop up to foul territory near third base.

Two outs, one to go.

And maybe the best little-league baseball player in the

world coming to the plate.

Then Andre noticed something: he could hear the wind in the trees, the fans murmuring behind him, Deets's feet in the dirt as he approached the plate.

He had forgotten to put the earplugs back in after batting last inning.

"Moment of truth," Deets said ominously and loudly enough for Andre to hear.

For a second, Andre wanted to call time and run to the dugout. Then he thought of something, snorted, and muttered something only Pat could appreciate:

"More like moment of 'goof.'"

Andre leaned forward and squinted like a gunfighter in the Old West. He took the sign and delivered the pitch. Deets swung and missed, and the crowd roared.

The pitcher threw again, and Deets fouled it straight back.

"Strike two!" the ump yelled.

Then Andre tossed a curveball, low and inside. Deets swung over top of it, but he caught just enough to send it along the ground into the infield.

A grounder! A dribbler to the shortstop! Who just happened to be their best defender!

Kevin bent to pick up the ball, ready to make the easy play at first, but it squirted under his glove and into the outfield. As Jayden ran to get it in shallow left, Deets turned at first base to go for two. He slid in safe, stood up on the bag, and popped his jersey for his dugout.

The Killington players went wild.

Instead of three outs and a loss, they now had a runner on second and the go-ahead run at the plate.

"Sorry, guys," Kevin fumed. "Sorry, Andre."

Andre shook his head to indicate no hard feelings, but now he had just three pitches left and suddenly felt made of stone. As he sized up Nada, the next hitter, he kept looking over his shoulder at Deets, worried he'd try to steal third.

Andre threw his first pitch. It was a ball, way outside.

Two pitches left.

He was determined to put the next one across, and Nada seemed to know it. As the fastball crossed the plate, the hitter smacked it out between first and second base on a rising line drive.

Mack saw it coming at him high and fast. He leaped and stretched his glove as far up as it would go. But the ball cleared it by a hair and didn't slow down as it fell toward the ground and out into the grass in shallow right field.

And Nelson.

"Deets is gonna head home. Nelson can't throw it that far!" Laker said queasily.

"No, but he can reach—" Hassan answered.

"The cutoff man!" Laker finished.

Before Mack had even landed from his jump, Andre was bolting past him and creating a target for Nelson to throw to.

"Hit me, New Money!" he yelled.

Just a week earlier, that name would have made Nelson cringe—now he felt it fill him with strength. He tracked the ball perfectly and moved to intercept it on the bounce. But the ball skipped higher than he'd expected on the dry ground and slammed hard into the heel of his glove—not the pocket.

"Oh!" the crowd groaned.

But to Nelson's surprise, it glanced straight up and seemed to hang in the air just above his head. He straightened up quickly, barehanded it, and fired it to Andre, now just about twenty-five feet from him.

The ball might not have even made it to the infield under its own power, but it was on target and the pitcher caught it cleanly. Just as Deets rounded third, Andre wheeled, reared back, and unleashed a throw to home that took him clear off his feet.

Andre landed on his stomach in the grass and watched the ball race Deets to the plate on a path that might as well have been a laser beam. Was it going to make it? Would it be too late? Andre technically wasn't thinking anything, but the voice in the back of his head repeated a single word: "Go."

Go, go, go, went the voice.

Still crouching in the dirt between first and second, Mack held his breath and watched with wide eyes as the ball flew by.

GO, GO, GO, GO, GO! his own voice echoed.

Pat stood with bent knees between home plate and Deets, who was barreling down the third-base line toward him. He braced for the impact of both the ball in his mitt and the future home run king on the rest of his body.

FWOP!

The ball landed in his mitt.

SMASH!

The home run king's shoulder landed on Pat's chest.

The two bodies tumbled past the plate. Pat skidded to a stop flat on his back, both hands held tight against his chest, while Deets frantically scanned the area around them and tried to answer the same question as everyone else on the field:

Where was the ball?

For a moment, no one breathed. Even Nada slowed to a trot as he rounded second, his eyes trained on the action—or lack thereof—at the plate.

The umpire took a step toward Pat, but he didn't need

a second. The catcher abruptly sat up, looked Deets directly in the face through the bars of his mask, and uttered a phrase the other boy had no chance of understanding:

"Lucky silver dollar, man."

Then he held his mitt aloft and plucked the baseball from it.

"You're out!" the umpire shouted.

Game over.

Camp Average 4, Killington 3.

What followed probably couldn't be called winning with class, but really, when would Camp Average have learned how to do that?

The crowd exploded in shrieks and cheers. Senior campers enveloped junior campers they didn't know in giant bear hugs. Laker and Hassan gave each other the longest series of consecutive high fives in recorded human history, and Winston bounded off the stands and into the outfield, both his hands in fists in the air.

Miles was the first Camp Average player to arrive at home plate. He tackled Pat into the dirt, a scream in his throat. Then Nelson jumped in, and the rest of the team followed suit.

All except Mack and Andre, who'd been mobbed by fans from the right-field bleachers before they could even stand up.

Their campmates raised them onto their shoulders and carried them toward the pile under the backstop, laughing and yelling the whole time.

"Hey, Mack!" Andre shouted over the noise.

"Yeah?"

"Wanna go swimming?"

Mack pumped his fist and pointed at his friend. "Now you're talking."

EPILOGUE

"CAN YOU EVEN IMAGINE?"

"Now you do the handshake line," Deets grumbled to Mack as the two teams passed each other at the pitcher's mound.

"Only sportsmanlike," Mack replied.

While most members of the Killington team hung their heads and lightly low-fived their opponents, the first baseman stopped to shake hands with each of them.

"See you around, I'm guessing," he told Andre. Then he looked Miles in the eyes and said, "Good game, Scorekeeper."

Soon the trophies had been handed out, the Killington players had slumped off to board their bus ... and the celebration began.

First, everyone ate burgers and hot dogs in the mess hall while Simon entertained them with the story of a new game: the one they'd all just watched.

"Andre had only a few pitches left in him, but we all believed he could pull it off. And hey—"

"We were due!" everyone shouted, already in on the new gags.

After dinner, the counselors turned on a movie, but nobody watched it. Even if they'd wanted to, who could have heard it over all the talking and laughing?

Instead, they continued the game recap while shoveling popcorn and chips into their mouths. The players recounted how they felt in certain moments, and Wi-Fi, Spike, and Mike told them what it was like in the stands—how they'd lost their voices from screaming and their hands ached from gripping their seats the entire game.

Miles passed around the scorecard, which he told everyone he was getting framed, and proudly pointed out the pencil scribbles representing his sacrifice bunt.

"Look," Miles said, pointing out Andre's three intentional walks. "Andre went one for one!"

"Just one measly at bat?" Pat said, deliberately missing Miles's meaning. "How about getting in the game next time, man?"

Andre laughed. "Hey, Pat, next time you catch a ball, can you not take an hour before showing us whether you've got it? Time is money."

Nelson leaped out of his chair. "Time is *New Money!*" he yowled incoherently, drawing groans from everyone but Pat, who gave him a fist bump.

"I knew I'd rub off on you eventually."

Everyone wanted to see Pat's lucky silver dollar, but he refused to take it out of his pocket.

"You'd probably just lose it," he said and turned up his nose. "Can you even imagine?"

Around midnight, the camp directors arrived to shut things down. As Simon walked from group to group, Winston stood in the doorway, arms crossed, surveying the room with a satisfied smile on his face.

"We don't expect you to be quiet right away," Winston shouted above the din, "but you should all be in bed in five minutes. Remember: early bird gets the win!"

Mack gave a look of disgust. "That's fine," he said under his breath. "I don't want to stick around if you're here anyway."

"Hey, whoa!" Andre countered as they exited the lodge through the side door with Laker and Brian in tow. It was a dark, clear night, and the path to their cabin was lit only by the bright spotlight on the camp office. "You're still mad at Winston? But we got our schedules back! And he was cheering harder than anybody."

Mack shook his head. "The ends don't justify the ... the ... DICTIONARY!"

"Nothing justifies the dictionary," Pat chimed in.

"I think you're looking for 'means,'" Miles offered. "The ends don't justify the means."

"Yeah," Mack said. "We won. We're happy. But we didn't need to be so unhappy to get here. I don't like the way he did things, and that doesn't change now."

"Maybe," Andre mused. "But we just beat Jeffrey Dietrich's nephew on his best day. I can't hold a grudge against anyone right now."

"And you get to go waterskiing tomorrow, Mack," Wi-Fi said.

"And Miles gets to do rocketry." Mack yawned. "Though why he'd want to is anybody's guess."

Just as they reached the cabin, he added a final thought: "And at least this means Winston's getting a new job somewhere else, so future Camp Average generations won't have to deal with him."

"He's not getting a new job somewhere else," Laker casually offered as he brushed past them up the stairs. "He's getting one *here*."

Mack felt his skin go cold. He and the other members of cabin 10 stopped dead in their tracks.

"As what?"

"Camp director. Like, *overall* camp director." Laker held open the door to the darkened cabin, rubbing his eyes. "Next summer, he's gonna be in charge of *everything*."